THE BANDIT LORD'S CAPTIVE

Alexa Ashe

The Bandit Lord's Captive

Copyright © 2023 by Alexa Ashe

All rights reserved.

No portion of this book may be reproduced, distributed, or transmitted in any form or by any means, including photocopying, recording, or other electronic or mechanical means, without the prior written permission from the publisher or author, except for the use of brief quotations in book reviews.

This book is a work of fiction. The characters and events in this book are fictitious. Any similarity to persons, living or dead, real or fictional, is purely coincidental and not intended by the author.

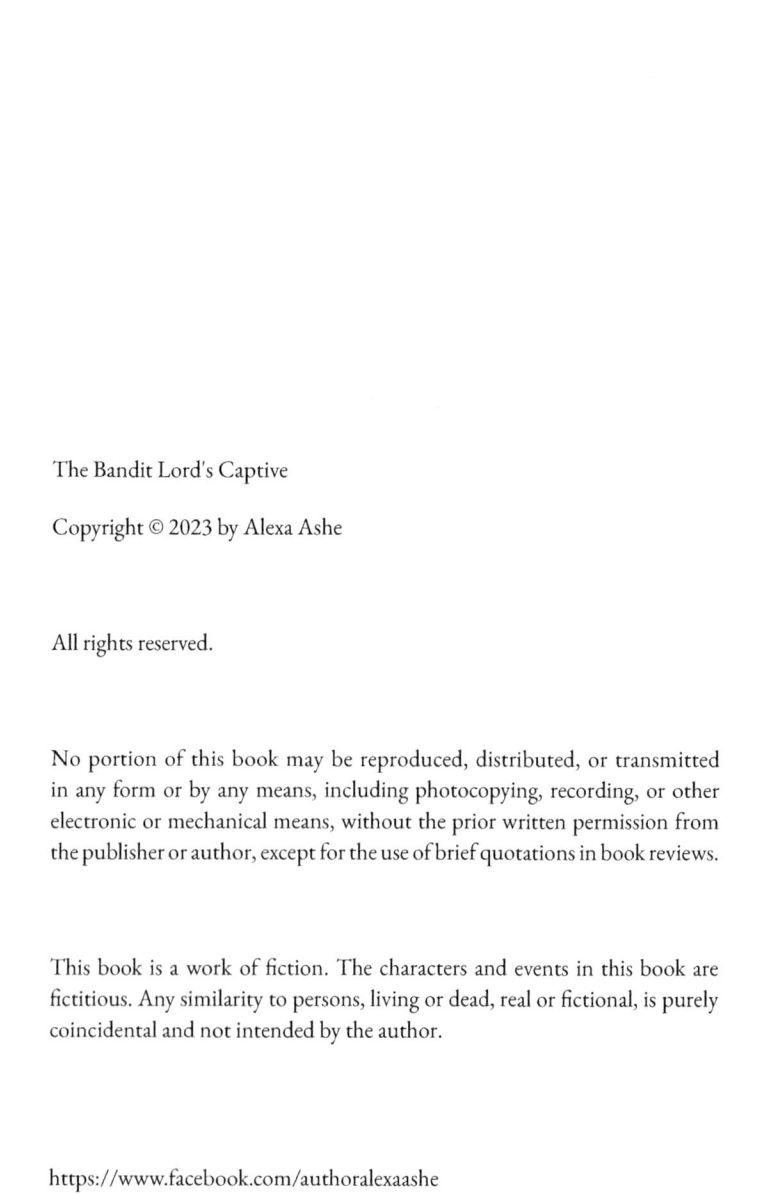

https://www.facebook.com/authoralexaashe

CONTENTS

1. Clio   1
2. Clio   9
3. Clio   14
4. Clio   22
5. Clio   28
6. Arthur   35
7. Clio   40
8. Clio   49
9. Clio   57
10. Clio   71
11. Arthur   76
12. Clio   81
13. Clio   89
14. Clio   100

15.	Clio	108
16.	Arthur	112
17.	Clio	117
18.	Clio	120
19.	Clio	129
20.	Arthur	140
21.	Clio	147
22.	Clio	157
23.	Arthur	163
24.	Clio	179
25.	Clio	183
26.	Clio	193
27.	Clio	198
28.	Clio	209
29.	Clio	215
30.	Clio	223
31.	Clio	229
What's next		234
Kell		237
Joula		242

About Author 250

Chapter One

CLIO

Everyone thinks they know me, but no one can see who I truly am.

They see a princess, the niece of the king, second in line to the throne, betrothed to the great Baron Leonas Ventiss. And yet, no one has ever stopped to ask me what I like, what my views on matters are, what my preferences are. They're all too busy loving and appreciating me. Like I'm not really a person—just a public figure for them to idolize. I often wonder what they'd think if they saw who I truly am.

I watch a flock of white birds flying over the bustling street, twisting toward the distant woods over the city wall. For a fleeting moment, I envy their freedom and the views they must see daily.

But my errand is not to daydream, so I turn away from the birds. I nod and smile at those I pass by, making excuses as to why I can't stop and chat or take their gifts. The bustling market street is busy this afternoon, which means I have to do this often and can't for a moment let the falseness of my smile show. It's a nuisance, to say the least.

The aroma of warm, fresh bread fills my senses as I take steps—ones trained into a gracefulness my whole life—up to the bread cart. I smile broadly at the balding old man, bent with age, who turns to me as I approach. His eyes widen subtly, as do most people's eyes when they first see me.

"Good morning to you, Master Helton," I say with a nod.

The old man's wrinkled features brighten. "A very blessed day to you, Princess. Good fortunes to you and yours."

"Please, Clio is just fine. It seems I'm unable to stop some people from calling me Lady De'Kalo. But I prefer Clio, if it's all the same to you."

Master Helton frowns with confused hesitation, likely trying to decipher my babbling, until he smiles again. "As you wish, Pr—ah, my Lady." He chuckles awkwardly, cheeks turning the faintest shade of pink. "I take it you're here for the festival? Word has it you're in charge of the arrangements this year."

I have to raise my voice to be heard over the roaring crowds, many of whom gather around the many other carts and stalls. One vendor in particular is yelling out their goods in an overly thunderous manner. He's loud enough for me to catch every word, and I know just how uninterested I am in the *almost new* bedrolls he's selling. I've never considered noise pollution to be an issue in the city, but perhaps it's something I should start paying attention to.

"I am here on festival duties, that is correct," I respond to the old man, and explain what baked goods I'd like for the event, reading from the list I made in my notebook.

The Kingdom of Aer will celebrate its one-hundred-and-forty-first year in only six days. Founding Festival is widely considered the highlight of the year, celebrated by all within the city's borders. Indeed, it's hard not to celebrate the glorious center of civilization. That's how the people of the Kingdom consider themselves, at least.

I still don't know what convinced me to organize the festival this year, but I'm happy to help my people celebrate. It's the least I can do to make myself feel useful.

"Don't you worry, my Lady," Master Helton says, noting down my order. "I'll have everything you need, to the best of my ability. It'll be my honor to be of service."

I give him a beaming smile. "You are very kind, good sir. I will be sure that your services and time are generously compensated."

He nods and grins humbly, bowing. We finish our arrangements, and I leave his stall, going about my next errands.

I keep my shoulders back and my head high, unflinchingly royal in everything I do, just as I was taught. I make sure to wave to anyone who notices me and bows, though I'm quickly distracted by a loud whistle that cuts through the air. The sharp, piercing sound startles me and causes me to tense my shoulders. Confused and worried murmurs ripple around me.

Down beyond where the street inclines ahead, we see soldiers in white uniforms racing towards the nearest city gate across the way. I eye their broadswords, long spears, and gleaming armor. The sight of the King's Guard in such a hurry twists my stomach.

"It's them. The Oathlanders," someone nearby says, which summons a fresh fear among the crowds.

"It's just a wolf or something," another says.

"They don't blow the whistle for a big dog at the gate," an elderly woman snaps fiercely. "Something's got them spooked."

"There hasn't been a war in over twenty years," a younger man replies. "No one would dare attack us."

A shiver washes over me. We can only wait and see what has alerted the palace guards. If it truly was an attack on the Kingdom, there would surely be more of an uproar. It likely is just a band of thieves or a mistaken threat.

And yet, we can't rule anything out. That's the life of a kingdom on the constant edge of war.

I continue down the street, nodding a hello to anyone who waves and greets me. I try to give them all a moment of focus. Then I notice the soot-stained young boy lurking in the shadows at the side of the street.

He can't be over ten years old, with a scrawny build under his weathered clothes and a mass of curly matted hair. A street dweller.

The city has come a long way towards solving our homeless issues, but even the Kingdom isn't perfect. It breaks my heart to see the poor boy looking so lost and hungry.

I pass by a fruit stall and ask for an apple, knowing the vendor will give me more than I ask for, as he always does. And with no charge.

True enough, he ends up giving me a small basket filled with fruit and some vegetables as a token of his appreciation for the royal family, and is blissfully unaware that not even the core of one apple will make it to the castle.

I thank him and stroll down the street, going around several groups who are still talking about the King's Guard being seen. With a warm smile and a nod, I leave the basket by the boy's feet and go on my way. When I look back, I see tears in his eyes as he grins broadly, snatching up the basket and disappearing from view.

Later that night, I'm in my suite in the royal palace, preparing a dinner for my father and fiancé. While I normally have cooks and bakers to tend to our meals, I've given them the evening off to allow myself time to cook, as I like to do from time to time.

I enjoy the peace it brings me, the way that none of my lessons can truly teach me this. A lot of it I've learned myself, because I wanted to and not because of who I am. The rest of what I know comes from kernels of information I've managed to squeeze from the cooks.

My father only arrived a few minutes ago and has already begun pouring us goblets of wine.

Royal Duke Markus De'Kalo is still wearing his crisp royal uniform, despite no longer having any official duties for the day. Although his beard is turning gray and his eyes have more wrinkles, he still moves with strength and grace of a man half his age. That's what a lifetime of training and discipline gets you.

We discuss the blowing of the King's Guard whistle earlier, and how it has been declared a false alarm. Someone reported spotting a group of bandits camping outside the city walls, but they'd been mistaken and they had found no one.

"Leonas won't be joining us this evening?" my father asks as he places my wine on the counter beside me.

"He's tending to his ordinance meetings," I say while I spoon garlic tomato sauce over the grilled chicken pieces. "He's running late, but said he'd make it in time for dinner."

"A time which has come, has it not?"

I give him a sideways glare. "*Almost* come. Give him time. He's a busy man."

My father nods, but it's clear he has more to say on the matter that he swallows down.

I know what he wants to say. My fiancé, Baron Leonas Ventiss, has been increasingly hard to find lately. I've noticed how little time we've been spending these past few months. Months that should have been spent planning our wedding. But I know how important he has become in the city's running since our betrothal, and I would not dare step in the way of his ambitions. Nor would I want him to stand in the way of mine.

"Something on your mind, petal?" my father asks, eyeing me over the rim of his goblet.

"Nothing at all," I say with a smile.

He doesn't seem convinced. "I would suggest you keep a better watch on your fiancé, seeing as you're meant to be in a partnership, but I know better than to meddle in your affairs."

"And yet I sense you're about to meddle," I grin.

"No meddling, I swear." He comes to stand beside me, regarding me with his dark hooded eyes. "I just wanted to remind you of your duties to the Kingdom. Of providing us heirs as soon as possible after your wedding, to fortify your marriage. However, it isn't that uncommon if you were to fall pregnant before the wedding. To ensure the ceremony still goes ahead."

My grin gone, I eye him warily, not liking how it sounds like I'm being pawned off, like some political game-piece.

I love my father and would do anything for my kingdom, but I don't like the tone in his voice or the suspicious way he's eyeing me. As if he doesn't fully trust my actions. Or he's afraid of them. I want to ask what is on his mind, but I'm too afraid to do so. Afraid of what he might say.

"I am marrying Leonas out of my love for him," I say. "And to allow us to gain his family's resources and influence across the waters."

My father swallows uncomfortably.

"Isn't that what you want to hear?" I ask.

Our eyes remain locked on each other for a moment. What is it he wants to tell me?

A blaring whistle pierces through the night air, making us both jump. The King's Guard is being summoned again. It's then I notice how light it is outside the windows.

We rush to the windows and see a fire raging in the street outside the castle walls.

People are calling out and rushing about in a panic. I can see a body on the ground.

An attack. The city is under attack.

Chapter Two

CLIO

I watch as the streets below fill with faceless masses, hidden within the darkness but illuminated by the growing flames.

The attackers look to be dressed in flowing cloaks and tunics, with hoods drawn low to hide their faces. They've broken through into the castle grounds and just below me there are breakouts of fights amidst flashing steel. A wall of fire is burning through the grounds to the side, making its way towards the castle.

The sight of my kingdom being terrorized tightens my chest and pounds my skull. Who would dare attack the Kingdom of Aer, and *why*?

My father rushed down to help gather the King's Guard and fight the attackers back, leaving me to stand and watch helplessly from afar. But when I see a group of city folk trapped behind a wall of flames, I feel the overwhelming urge to go help them.

I'm heading out of my suite before I know it, bunching my skirts up as I run down the carpeted steps and make my way out the front doors. The cacophony of battle hits my senses, as does the heat from the fires. The night sky is alive with death and terror.

King's Guard in their gleaming white armor rush by me, likely oblivious to their Princess being so close to the fighting.

I hear one soldier call out, "They're heading for the gold depository!"

Is that what's going on? I wonder. *All this to steal our gold?*

I have no time to dwell on that as I make my way to people trapped behind the fire. My stomach leaps into my throat when I see a bandit charging towards me with a sword drawn, but he's stopped when an arrow from above pierces his throat. Like the others, he's dressed in weathered cloaks and simple clothing that gives him a foreign look. I try to ignore the chaos all around as I near the wall of flames, the air burning and smothering.

There appears to be a family on the other side of the flames. They're backed up into a corner with the fire slowly spreading towards them and up the stone walls. Near them is a wooden structure holding a ladder that reaches up to the higher battlements.

I get an idea to try to pull apart a section of the crisscrossing beams, hoping to loosen the structure. Then I shove against a beam, aiming to topple the structure into the flames. But it doesn't budge. I shove and yell with all my might, my shoes slipping against the ground, but I can only shift the beams slightly.

Cries of pain and death ring out all around. In the distance, I see a body on fire, running about against the darkness. Chills ripple through me. I fear for my father and fiancé, but there's little I can do for them right now. I must save these people.

With renewed strength, I push against the beams with my shoulder, my face twisting with effort. The flames are so hot and stifling.

A white light flashes in my vision. The beams shift, and suddenly the structure begins to topple. Beams and boards crash down into the fire, smothering most of it. It's enough to allow the family to run out for safety. They thank me as they go, but my mind is now on that white light I thought I'd seen. My guess is that it had been lighting from above, or possibly a flaming arrow cutting through the sky. But I'm not sure, and the feeling of uncertainty troubles me.

Down the street, the King's Guards charge towards a cluster of bandits, who I'm surprised to see are running away. Are the attackers truly fleeing? I've never been in any situation like this, so I can't tell if we're winning or losing.

My heart is pounding as I look over the dark figures of fallen bodies strewn about. There's a line of blood splashed over the ground nearby. A scream fills the air, and I look up to see a uniformed soldier falling from the castle tower. I quickly turn away before he hits the ground, but I can't help but look back to see the crumpled heap of a body.

So much death and destruction.

I turn to find safety back inside the castle, feeling too exposed out in the open like this. But before I get far, I hear the cries of a child. After a moment, I find the young girl, no more than five, standing in the back of a wagon. She's crying ferociously.

Without thinking, I rush away from the castle and towards the wagon. It won't take me long to help the girl. She must have been separated from her family in the chaos.

Two King's Guards charge by me towards the nearest fleeing bandits. My path takes me to the side of the castle to the east exit, where there's less commotion.

When I get to the wagon, I see four horses standing idle by the reins at the front and reach out for the girl.

"It's okay," I say. "Come here."

She steps back and shakes her head, tears streaming down her cheeks. I urge her to come to me, but she's frozen with fear. "Father!" she cries, in an accent I can't quite place.

"Alright, then. I'll come to you." I step onto a large wheel and hop into the cargo bed. The metal creaks under my feet as I land. I step around some crates and say to the girl, "It's okay. Just put your arms around me, and we'll get out of here."

Once I'm close enough, it's easy for her to wrap her arms around me. She's whimpering and shaking, and looks completely lost. It feels good to pick her up in my arms.

I reach the end of the cargo bed and ease her down to the ground. My heart aches for her when she instantly reaches out for me to keep holding her. Within the chaos all around, I hear thudding footsteps.

Dark figures are approaching the wagon, coming from the castle grounds. I duck low and wave the girl away.

"Go. Hide. Get to safety. I'll come for you," I whisper urgently.

She's still frozen for a second until the figures get closer, their swords glinting in the low light. Then she turns and runs as fast as her little legs can carry her to the shadows by a wall and hides behind some barrels.

I move to jump out too, but it's too late to not be seen, so I back up to stay out of sight as the men reach the wagon. I can't see who they are, but I hear them scramble into the front carriage and yell at the horses to go. They're grumbling to each other, but I can't make out anything they're saying.

Curled up between the crates, I grab a blanket and cover myself just as two men climb into the back. From the accents of their hurried, gruff voices, I know they're not King's Guards.

The wagon takes off, and I have no choice but to stay hidden. If the bandits see me, I'll surely be killed.

Chapter Three

CLIO

My heart feels like it's going to burst out of my chest as I lie hidden under the dense blanket. I don't know what's happening, but I feel the swaying of the wagon, the horse's hooves hitting the ground, and the occasional whispering among the outlaws. If they find me, I'll surely be killed. Or worse.

I can't believe I let myself get into this mess.

I only hope that someone from the Kingdom will have seen me go into the back of the wagon and is now pursuing these bandits. It's just a matter of time before they rescue me. If not, I don't know how I'm going to get myself out of this. That little girl I saved likely won't be much help if anyone even knows to question her.

From what I can hear of the talk amongst the bandits, they've suffered several losses, and a few people are missing. They speak little for a long while. I'm going to take a guess and say that it didn't go nearly as well as they'd hoped.

My first thought was that these are the Wildmen I've heard stories about. They live in the Wildlands far out of the city, deep in the wilderness. But the Wildmen are uncivilized cannibals who have their own guttural language, according to history books. These men sound fairly educated, possibly even civilized.

After what must be at least two hours, the wagon finally stops. I stay where I am, hardly daring to breathe, let alone move. There is some talk among the bandits, but again, it's hard to hear exactly what they're saying.

Someone hops back into the cargo bed, shaking the wagon. I hold my breath, not wanting to call any attention to myself, but a moment later, my blanket is ripped away.

A frightened squeal escapes me as I curl up as small as I can. It's dark and at first it is hard to see the faces of the men standing around me. The sword pointed at my face is very clear to see, however. Dark, ragged silhouettes of trees loom overhead, highlighted by the milky glow of the moon.

"Well, well, look what we have here," one bandit growls.

"Very nice, indeed," another says, his eyes roaming my skirt and blouse.

Rough hands pull me out of the wagon, and someone ties my hands behind me with a rough length of rope. I stand there, looking over my kidnappers as my eyes adjust to the moonlight.

Despite their roughness with me, the men look relatively presentable, with a spark of intelligence in their eyes. I am sure they aren't Wildmen. The weathered clothing makes it hard to tell who these strangers are, but I can tell that the weapons they have with them are of a high quality. As much as I know about such things, at least.

"Isn't this a pleasant surprise?" a bandit chuckles. Like the others I've heard so far, he's well spoken, if a little rough around the edges. "Where's Fireheart?"

"Here he is," another man answers.

A tall, broad-shouldered man steps through them, coming to me. The sight of him quickens my heart. He reminds me of a stalking predator; every movement calculated. The intense look he's giving me makes me feel like he can see right through my defenses.

"How did you come to be with us?" he asks, his voice low and hinting at subtle power.

"I didn't mean to," I say, knowing there's no use in making up a story. "I was just trying to get to safety and ended up hiding in the back when your men returned to the wagon. I... didn't know what else to do but hide."

He's clearly in charge among them, and so I treat him as such. I try to plead with him with my eyes.

"What'll we do with her, sir?" a bandit asks.

The tall man, who the other bandit referred to as Fireheart, gazes at me intently. "We keep her for now." His brows draw together. "Who are you?"

"No one," I quickly say, perhaps a little too quickly. "I'm... my mother is a cook in the Royal Castle. I live there."

He eyes me with suspicion, his gaze cutting into me as if trying to uncover my secrets. "Your clothes are not befitting a cook's daughter and that necklace is more valuable than a Lord's estate. How did you come by such riches?" His voice is harsh and accusing.

"She's a cloudhead," someone says. "They all dress like they're about to host a god."

That gets some chuckles from the other men hidden in the darkness. That name isn't familiar to me, but I can tell it isn't flattering.

"Maybe we caught their Queen," a voice among them says.

"Idiot, they don't have a Queen," says another.

"I reckon she is just some palace peasant. Probably worthless to us. I say we kill her and leave her here."

"That'll leave a trail for them to follow us."

"Enough," the tall man says, firmly enough to cut through the chatter. His words carry a strong sense of authority, as if he is accustomed to being heard and obeyed. "We keep her for now. It matters little who she is. We need to keep moving. Finish up and we keep going for a few more hours."

I notice some among them are tending to wounds, wrapping bandages and rubbing ointments on cuts.

The way they're all looking at me disgusts me. None of them sees who I truly am, just like everyone in the Kingdom. They see who they want to see. Whoever they want me to be. It would matter little if they knew my name and status; they'd still think of me however they want and make up their own judgements.

These bandits carry themselves like soldiers, although they're certainly not dressed like any military I've ever seen. Could they be from Koprus, the city to the south? I'm not aware of any grievances they would have with the Kingdom of Aer, but perhaps they're looking to overthrow the center of civilization? Others have tried in the past, like the Oathlanders and the Syraxies.

"Watch her at all times," the tall man says to two men standing by me.

For a moment longer, my eyes remain locked with his own, which burn like twin coals of intense heat, before he turns his attention to the other bandits.

His features are chiseled as if from marble and bear a ferocious expression; with broad shoulders, a rugged jawline, and a scowl that seems perpetually etched on his face. His dark hair is pulled back and his beard is well kept. His powerful gaze conveys such lucidity and alertness that the slightest movement seems to draw his attention, and his clothing is aged yet of high-quality. He doesn't talk as much as the others, but seems to speak with his eyes.

I shiver against the chill of the night. I hadn't realized how cold it would be out in the wilderness, wherever we are. This could be any of the forests outside of the city.

Something crunches in the undergrowth, startling me. I immediately imagine beasts lurking in the darkness. But my spirits lift when I consider it could be soldiers from the Kingdom, searching for me. Could my saviors be here already? Hope fills my chest and my heart beats a little faster.

But I see no one within the surrounding darkness, and nothing moving by the glow of the moonlight.

Did my father live through the attack? Did the king? My fiancé was across the city at the time of the attack, but perhaps he had gone to defend the palace. My mind races with troubled thoughts that pound my skull. The cool night air sends another shiver through me.

This must be the furthest I've ever been from the city. Though that wouldn't really be hard to beat, since I don't think I've been more than an hour away in any direction before. I've never been important enough to leave, but always important enough to have to stay.

The night sky is alive above me, a roiling sea of misty forms and glittering lights. I'm amazed at how bright it is, and how an explosion of stars sparkles like a million fireflies. The beauty of the heavens is so vibrant that it overwhelms my senses and takes my breath away, with this expansive stardust spilling through the gaps between the trees. The Kingdom is usually so overblown with light that I hadn't even known how much of the night sky it was hiding.

"Must be a little clearer than you're used to," a deep voice says, startling me from my thoughts.

The tall man has come up to me again, his movements now calm and controlled, and if he's trying not to spook me. He towers above me, easily reaching six-and-a-half feet tall, compared to my petite frame.

It's almost as if he'd been reading my thoughts. He stands beside me and looks up. "I heard that there are places in your city where the buildings are so close together that some people in your city rarely see the night sky in all its glory. If you ask me, that's more of a crime than half of the laws that are voted in."

I'm not sure how to respond to that, but I manage to say, "It's one of the most beautiful sights I've ever seen." The honesty in my voice surprises me. This feels like a very odd moment to have with the leader of the men who have me captive.

He points to a cluster of stars. "You see how these ones join together in a curve? That's called the Blade of Coz. You know, the God of War?"

"We know who the God of War is in the Kingdom," I say, sounding sharper than I intended.

He ignores my bluntness and points to another cluster, this one made up of several stars that cover much of the sky. I'm still not sure why he's spending time with me.

"This one here," he says, pointing at the array of stars, "is the Maiden and the Monster."

"Like the children's tale," I say.

"Like the children's tale." He pauses for a moment, as if considering his next words. "But the story does not tell the truth of what occurred. They have watered it down over the centuries for childish tastes. The actual story is that it was the maiden who seduced the man and cursed him into a monster."

I shake my head. "I'm sorry, but that is simply nonsense. The tale is simply a made-up story for children to listen to while they fall asleep. The maiden and the monster, despite their differences, fell in love and lived happily ever after. It's a bedtime tale."

His dark eyes burn into me. "You should not believe everything you hear, my lady."

"I am no Lady," I quickly say, hoping it sounds believable. The last thing I want is for these men to realize I might be a bargaining chip for them. I refuse to be used against my country.

"Every woman is a lady." The sincerity in his tone takes me by surprise. Then he doubles my confusion by untying my hands. He takes a cloth that's been dipped in ointment from another man and nods to the scratches on my forearm. Scratches I haven't even noticed before.

"Tend to yourself," he says, and leans closer. "We will bind you again once you clean your wounds, but you do not need to fear for your safety when you're with us. I give you my word on that. However, if you attempt to escape, I will personally remove your head and leave it for your Kingdom folk to find."

With that, he turns away from me and calls out for them to keep moving. I'm left shaking with nerves, my heart racing.

Something tells me I should fear this man more than I've feared anything else in my life.

Chapter Four

CLIO

We continue through the wilderness all night long. I sit in the back of the wagon again, with my hands tied uncomfortably behind me. Four men sit around me, and three are up front on the bench. Others are riding horses or in other wagons. There must be over forty men among them. No women.

I wonder how many of them attacked the city and how many fell. It was foolish for so few bandits to attack such a well-protected city, anyway. Had it been an assassination attempt? Purely an attempt to steal our gold? A distraction for something else? My brain hurts trying to piece out the truth about the confusion of the night.

The bandits must have been instructed not to talk to me, and they say little for some time.

We travel throughout the next day, stopping to rest and eat, or to rest briefly for some sleep. I'm grateful for the small scraps of bread and cheese they give me, although they can hardly be considered hospitable hosts. The day is mild, thankfully, with little wind and a good amount of sun when it isn't overcast.

I keep thinking about what the tall man said, about me being safe with them, but that he'd behead me if I tried to escape. If I believe in the second part of that, I must believe the first is also true.

As they set up camp the next night, several bandits keep watch. I've been constantly looking back to check if anyone from the Kingdom pursues us, waiting for the moment I see a battalion of soldiers charging at us.

I also watch their leader when I think no one is looking. What had they called him? Fireheart? An odd name, for sure. But then, perhaps that is a common name from wherever they're from. He hasn't spoken to me since his warning. Hardly even looked my way.

The farther we travel, the more I can rule out some lands as our destination, and the more confused I get. We've crossed through a vast forest, which could have been the Willowwood, and that would have us traveling east. But the two rivers we've crossed could be north, east, or south of the Kingdom, from what I can remember from the maps. I've never been one for traveling or knowing things like how to tell your position from the sun or the shadows, like some of the King's Guard I've known.

I have to wonder why these people traveled so far just to steal some gold.

While the bandits rest and eat their rations for the evening, I hear something shifting around us. Something large moving through the bushes, crunching twigs. Then the sounds stop.

Several of the men look spooked.

"Do you think..." one says, and mouths the word *Wildmen*.

"Not around here," someone says, a large knife in his hand.

"How do you know? We've all heard the stories. Civilized folk gone mad, going around eating people. They're so far gone they don't even talk like people anymore."

"The Wildlands are deep to the north," someone else says. "Nowhere near our position."

One of them points a half-eaten potato on a fork at him. "You almost sound like you know what you're talking about."

A shiver runs through me at the thought of being discovered by the Wildmen out here. I can hardly believe that people have turned into such savages, if the stories are really to be believed. But these bandits seem to believe in them enough. Perhaps they've even seen the Wildmen before.

When we continue the next morning, moving before the sun rises, I try to picture the maps in my head. My gut tells me we're heading east, and there are no established settlements this far east of the Kingdom, except for one. And that fills me with a dread that trembles at my core.

My head is weary from traveling, my hands aching from being tied for most of the day, my clothes are filthy and I'm in dire need of a bath. On top of that, I'm desperate for something good to eat. Even something small that isn't stale bread and cheese.

Our second night at camp, I ask one of the kinder-looking bandits if I can have something to eat, particularly the dried beef they're chewing on. Even if it does smell a bit off.

"I can give you something to eat," the man says, and grabs his crotch.

Others nearby burst into laughter.

"I have eaten nothing since the morning. All day," I say. "Please."

The men seem to take pleasure at my plight. I look for the one in charge of them, but he's nowhere to be seen. I'm not even sure if he'll be more responsive than these men.

"I can give her something, for sure," one of them says, leering at me. "Out here, no one would know."

"I'll go next, since she'll no doubt still have an appetite after you," another says, which sends them into more laughter.

I'm all-too aware of being the only woman among a large group of men. Out in the rolling hills between civilizations. The way some of them are looking at me causes a tightness in my chest and seizes my throat. I know then that I won't be asking for food again. Hell, I won't even let myself sneeze to keep their attention off of me.

I hardly sleep that night, waiting for an assault that never comes. I stop trying to communicate with any of them and just keep hoping to survive this ordeal. I'm no longer waiting for anyone to come rescue me.

It isn't until the sunset of the next day that we reach our destination.

We head towards a large town with simple huts for houses on the outskirts, and a built-up area in the center with taller structures. There are fields with livestock and people tending to their crops. The town is surrounded by rolling hills and cliff faces, with buildings on multiple levels, all squeezed close together. It's nothing like the grand swooping scale of the Kingdom, but feels more like a big country town to me. It's hard to see in great detail with the setting sun fading and bathing everything in a golden red glow.

I've never seen so many levels and layers in a town before; a place embedded in the land's structure. But I have seen depictions of such a place. And that fills me with crippling dread.

I finally know where I'm being taken, and I realize I should have known all along. A part of me, deep down, knew where I was going, but finally seeing the truth is a fresh horror.

This is the Oathlands. The sworn enemy of the Kingdom of Aer. I'm in the hands of the enemy.

I do not speak and try to hide how frightened I am. I can only await my fate.

Once we're in the town, a small group of the men and their leader take me up hundreds of steps carved into the rock, to a black tower at the top of a cliff wall. This tower is away from the tightly packed center of the town.

The Oathlands have no king or queen, and as far as I know, they're led by their military. But this tower with its jagged spires and twisting architecture looks like a place of command. A tower to look out over others in town.

It's been decades since anyone from the Kingdom has set foot in the Oathlands, so perhaps they've since found a new ruler.

I'm taken to a prison cell in the tower. A cold square room made of rock, with no windows and little light coming through the bars of the cell door. I'm just discarded like unwanted trash. It doesn't seem to bother anyone that I haven't eaten for a day and a half.

I try to hold on to the hope that my father or someone from the Kingdom will come to rescue me, but it's a fool's hope, and I know deep down that I'm likely going to die here as a prisoner.

Chapter Five
CLIO

It feels like early morning when someone comes to retrieve me from my cell. Despite my exhaustion, I found it impossible to sleep on the stone floor and I feel sick all over. My head is pounding and my muscles are aching as I follow the guards out into the hallway. I've never felt so filthy or been so disheveled before. I contemplate whether I would murder one of these guards for a hot bath and a good meal. I doubt I'll get such luxuries in the hands of the enemy, though.

The carpeted hallways are sparse, giving little personality away, and the two uniformed guards have little to say to me. I follow them through double doors to a large room with a long dining table in the center. There are paintings on the walls –of people and landscapes that I assume are parts of the Oathlands.

I still can't believe I'm actually in the land of the sworn enemy of the Kingdom. A place where savages live. Although this tower, and what I saw of the town yesterday, doesn't exactly seem like the place of savages.

"You may sit and eat," one guard says stiffly. They remain on either side of the doors and wait for me to enter the room.

I reach the long table and see there are plates of meat pies and buttered bread beside a tankard of water. Despite my hunger, I find it difficult to feast while in captivity. I desperately want to sip the water, but I can't trust these people. So I sit there until a door on the other side of the room opens.

The leader of the bandit group strides in, and I raise my brows at the sight of him. He's almost a new man now, in a crisp buttoned uniform, shiny knee-high boots, and his skin and hair freshly washed. He almost looks regal. I'm taken by how striking he looks, despite the fear that courses through me.

I will personally remove your head and leave it for your Kingdom folk to find. His words, and the intensity behind them, will never leave my mind.

"Please, help yourself," he says, gesturing to the food and water. "I meant it when I said you do not need to fear for your safety." He takes a seat a few chairs away from where I am at the head of the table.

I remain unmoving. "And did you also mean what you said about removing my head?"

He almost looks uncomfortable, his cool façade breaking for the first time. "I apologize. That was perhaps a tad dramatic. But I didn't want you running off and coming to harm out in the wilds. Or causing problems for me and my men. Please, you must be starving and weary. I swear, the food and drink are safe for consumption."

I keep my eyes on him as I take a buttered slice of bread, and am surprised at how soft and doughy the bread is. I pause with the bread partway to my mouth. "I cannot eat with someone just watching me like that."

A slight smile begins to form on his lips as he piles food onto the plate in front of him.. "Fair point."

The bread is one of the best things I've ever tasted, and the thickly spread salted butter is divine. But that's likely because of my starvation. I greedily pour the water straight from the tankard into my parched mouth, not caring that some spills onto my chin and blouse, and splatters onto the wooden table.

"My name is Arthur Bearon," he says. "And your name?"

What do I tell him? "Wendy," I say.

He gives me a look that tells me he doesn't believe that. "Well, whoever you are. I must tell you that I didn't mean for you to be kidnapped. We clearly didn't know we had a stowaway until it was too late to return you. I was left with no choice but to bring you with us. While that does make you a sort of prisoner here, I don't want you to think of it that way."

"A... freedom-lacking guest?" I suggest.

That brings another small grin to his lips, hidden under his beard. "I'm sure there is a better way to put it than that. Please, try the *firousa*."

I stare at him blankly.

"The meat pie," he says, gesturing. "I believe you also make it with rabbit and deer."

I eye the meat pies before me. They look similar to what I know, with the same round disc shape and crusty top. "You mean a *grossa* pie. The name comes from when they were so common that there were grosses of them."

"We are talking about the same thing. Just with a different name. You see, our ways and customs are not so different to yours. We're not the animals and heathens you think us to be."

He watches while I take a careful bite of the pie. It's cold and a little stale, but not tasteless. I notice him scrutinizing me.

"Red hair is not so common in the Kingdom, is it not?" he asks.

I instinctively touch my messy hair. "It isn't *uncommon*," I say, but the truth is that red hair is indeed rare in the Kingdom. There are many with light brown, orange, and dark auburn hair, though few with the brightness of my red.

I set down the pie and stare at him firmly. "If you're going to kill me, then I wish it to be done sooner than later."

His angled brows draw together slightly. "You have the wrong impression of me. And my people."

"Your people? So you rule them?"

"No. No one rules us. I simply want what's best for us, and they recognize that"

"And is that to start another war? Is that what's best for you all?" I hold his gaze challengingly. I know what I know and I won't have a foreign abductor telling me what to think.

I raise my chin a little higher and continue, "Our people have been at war for centuries. We've lost countless lives on both sides. I'm sure you have your side of things and we have ours. But it's not possible to say who is right or wrong in such matters, after so much bloodshed. There was an unspoken agreement to leave each other alone. After the Last Blood War, we stayed away, and you, in turn, stayed in your place. That's why we've had peace for over twenty years."

This was back when I was just a baby, and I grew up hearing the stories of the last war and how there was a tentative truce between societies. That truce had grown stronger with each passing year, until it reached a point where peace became an accepted part of life.

"You know so much," he says, lowering his brows. "I'm sure there's no convincing you of anything otherwise."

"You can try all you like, but I won't believe any of what you say. Is that why you brought me here? To show me you aren't savages who've waged war against for centuries?"

"You have your views," he says, "because they've been teaching you lies in your precious kingdom. Your King De'Kalo is a usurper. *We* are the rightful rulers of the entire kingdom. But they'd never teach you that in your history. Your kingdom has changed history to suit its own agenda."

I'm speechless for a moment, but I don't believe a word he's saying. "For all I know, you're teaching your people the history you want to believe in. I believe my country's word over that of the man who holds me captive."

The thought of this Oathlander challenging my kingdom's purity rattles me, quickening my pulse. "There is one major difference between our people. We would never treat someone we called a guest like the way I've been treated. Kingdom folk have hearts and souls, while you Oathlanders are heartless and have no capacity for love.

"You, sir, are a coward for attacking our city. How many died because of your greed for our gold? You said I was safe with you, but that didn't stop your men from threatening to assault me. I couldn't sleep for one second knowing they could have their way with me whenever they wanted, and for all I knew, you would be the ringleader, goading them on."

My temples are burning hot and I have enough anger in me to barely register his confused and somewhat troubled expression. I just keep going, unable to convince myself to shut my mouth. "You Oathlanders are empty shells of people who don't understand what it means to care or to love. I don't expect you to know anything about that. You and your people are no better than the Wildmen. In fact, I believe you Oathlanders are the same as those uncivilized, feral inhumans. That is what I truly believe. I will not be spoken to by a heartless man who—"

He slams his hands on the table. "Enough!"

The sudden action snatches the breath from me.

"I've heard enough from that mouth of yours," he says, his shoulders heaving and eyes glittering with anger. "Send her back to her cell immediately," he adds to the guards.

Before I can say anything else, I'm escorted back to my cold, dark cell. Back to being a prisoner. To think of how unhinged my captor had become. He might have been pleasant briefly, but I remind myself I have no idea what kind of a man he is, or what he's capable of.

Chapter Six
Arthur

"Now that the cussing and insults are out of the way, would you mind telling me what in all the hells you were thinking, brother?"

I stare at Rourk, searching for my words, but all I can do is shake my head. We've been yelling at each other for the better part of an hour, with me trying to justify entering the Kingdom of Aer with our soldiers, and him telling me how I've doomed us all. We're both exhausted and the red in our faces is slowly fading.

We will spend the rest of our evening drinking wine and being a little more civilized, so I pour us two glasses.

"I still cannot believe you managed to steal fifty of my men," Rourk says, taking the armchair across from mine. He rubs the weariness on his face with frustration. "They're all going to be court-martialed tomorrow. Every one of them who returned. Those you didn't send to their deaths."

"It's not their fault," I say, sitting with a grunt. It's been an exceptionally long few days. "The blame should fall on my shoulders alone. I convinced them to do what's best for our people, and they willingly followed me, honestly believing we were doing the right thing."

Rourk's dark eyes flash. "And attacking our sworn enemy was the right thing to do?"

"I've told you we never meant to attack," I say with some heat in my voice, which I have to bite back. "We only meant to sneak in undetected, to take their seeds and grains. Instead, they mistook our intentions and thought we were after their gold."

Rourk sighs harshly and takes a big gulp of his wine. I study my brother, wondering on the best tact to use on him. While we share the same sharp nose, hooded brows, and dark eyes, my older brother has always opted for longer hair and a clean-shaven face.

The tension in his eyes tells me he's feeling the weight of our society on his shoulders. It's a look I recognize from my own anxieties.

"In all that's good and mighty, Arthur, did you really think you'd get away with this?"

"Our town is slowly dying," I tell him, knowing we've had this conversation countless times already. "We're going to run out of resources eventually unless we do something about it *now*, before it's too late. Our fields and crops are dying. We're running out of *food*. And that's a fact you can't deny. What would you have me do? Sit here in my tower and watch our town rot?"

"Instead of sitting here doing nothing, you decided to start another war with the Kingdom." His voice is low and filled with resigned damnation.

"They have nothing that points towards us. We were completely unmarked."

"They'll *know*, Arthur. They'll know. Even if they have no proof, they'll look to us. And you should have known this."

"I considered leaving a falstine leaf from Koprus for them to find. Or a torn cloth the color of Syraxia maroon and navy. But I couldn't bring myself to send a war to anyone's doorstep."

"You have some good sense in you, at least," Rourk says, sipping his wine. "We have to expect a retaliation, though. We have to. Sooner or later, the Kingdom will come snooping around here. If they don't come in full attack force."

"They don't want another war as much as we don't."

"They don't care for war because they know they'll win, and they know we know it. It's boring for them. Their army is three times the size of ours. We're the ones who don't want another war because we know it might mean we'll get wiped out."

I sip my wine contemplatively. Our land is slowly dying, the flowers losing their bloom and grass no longer sprouting, and while we have some livestock remaining, it isn't enough to sustain us much longer. Our forecasts say we have a couple of years at most before we reach dire circumstances.

If I could have just retrieved some seeds and grains, or perhaps a bit of their gold, it would have given us decades more of a bountiful life. The reward outweighed the risk for me. After all of our scouting and observations of the Kingdom, there was no way for me to know our attempt would have gone so wrong.

I'm still not sure how that fire had broken out. A local coming across us and getting spooked, perhaps? Tipping over a lantern in the wrong place. It's hard to say exactly how things had gone so wrong so quickly.

"Those twelve souls are on me," I say solemnly. "I will personally with each of their families and explain what happened. They will hate me. Not you."

"There you go, playing the martyr, again," Rourk says, shaking his head. "I swear, I think that's why they love you so much. The hero of the Oathlands. Fireheart. Our silent guardian. Or whatever they call you."

"The silent guardian is a new one," I say. "Do you think it's because I don't talk much?"

Rourk cocks an eyebrow. "Well, you do play the silent brooding card a lot."

"We can't all have your winning personality," I retort. That gets me a small smirk from him.

I can tell the tension is easing from him now that we've been talking more, but he's far from satisfied. I don't think he ever will be. Losing lives is never acceptable.

As the General Commander of the Oathlands Military, my brother knows he's going to have to deal with a lot after what I've done. I've always been in good favor with the Grandmaster General, and with Rourk as his second-in-command, hopefully between the two of us we can prevent the Grandmaster from overreacting or doing anything brash, like starting a war with the Kingdom before they start one with us.

There are two things I'm not telling my brother.

First is that not all of the twelve soldiers were known to be killed. Four of them are unaccounted for, but presumed dead. There was even an extra member in our squad which I also don't tell him about.

And I also won't dare tell him I have a captive from the Kingdom. I have yet to figure out who I have in my basement cell. All I know is that her name is not Wendy, as she claimed. She's a terrible liar. I must learn more about my prisoner.

No, Arthur. Not your prisoner. That's not the way I should be looking at it. I'm going to have to be very delicate with her, if I'm going to get any information from her.

I still can't believe how infuriating she'd been earlier this evening. How angry she'd made me. But that was on me. Somehow, she'd found exactly the right way to light my fuse. It's been a while since anyone has made me feel anything on that level.

"I just need to figure out what I'm going to tell Darius tonight," Rourk says. "This can't wait until morning. I'm going to get all the hells for this."

"I'll come with you."

"You've done enough, brother. It's best you're not there to stoke his fire when I tell him what's happened. Our Grandmaster can be... hot tempered, at the best of times, to say the least."

I nod, falling into thought. Have I doomed us all by my reckless actions? Will the Kingdom come for my captive?

Right now, I feel the most important thing I can do is to determine who I have in my cell. Who is behind those deep-blue eyes and that stubborn face?

And why can't I stop thinking about her?

Chapter Seven

CLIO

The jarring of the cell doors opening shocks me awake. I feel dead. I have no concept of what time it is, but I think it's either late morning or early afternoon, judging by the cripplingly bright light in the hallway beyond my prison.

I've managed to sleep but somehow feel much worse for it. My muscles are sore and stiff, and my head is throbbing violently.

"Lord Bearon has requested your company for breakfast," one of the two guards says.

I feel half delirious as I'm escorted out of the cell. I think they're different from the two guards who had brought me in there the night before. But, in their tan buttoned shirts, crisp black trousers and black boots, they each blend into another without focusing on their faces.

They called him Lord Bearon? I wonder as I walk, trying to keep myself from collapsing. *That's new.*

I'm sent back to what I call the dining hall. My gracious host, the smug know-it-all Lord Bearon, is already there at the long table. He's sitting at the end of the table, where I'd sat the night before.

He's in a crisp shirt that shows off his powerful shoulders and broad chest, and trim black trousers. It's a fairly casual attire, but then I am used to nobles and royals on a daily basis.

"How did you sleep?" he asks as I walk up to the table.

I glare at him. "I was in a prison cell. How do you think?" I pause and consider the seats at the table. "Did I take your favorite seat last night?" I ask.

I'm mindful of how much I reek in my dirt and sweat-stained clothes, which I've been wearing for four days now. So I take a seat several chairs away from him. His watchful gaze hasn't left my face, but he ignores my question.

The long table has an array of options. There are cinnamon scrolls, a large platter of fruit, scrambled eggs, sausages, and several kinds of breads and pastries. It all smells absolutely heavenly and makes my stomach rumble. There are also tankards of fresh juice and water.

My eyes light up at the sight and smell of fresh hot coffee. Its aroma is slowly wafting from a jug.

I sit down, trying to control my desperate cravings and not give away how weak I am.

"May I ask for your real name?" he says.

"I told you," I say. "It's Wendy."

"Just Wendy?"

"Wendy... Allspice," I say challengingly, daring him to doubt me.

He smirks at that. His eyes lock onto mine and for a moment I struggle not to get lost in his dark, brooding eyes. There is something about him that is compelling and captivating, and that troubles me greatly. He is likely used to getting his way and controlling people. I won't allow myself to be manipulated.

The plate before me is flanked by a silver knife and fork. I decide to trust the food before me. If he wanted to kill me, he would have done so by now, rather than waiting to poison me.

I take a deep breath. "I want you to know that I'm normally a lot more lady-like. However, considering the situation..."

I grab a sausage and finish it in three quick bites. Then I pop several apple and melon chunks in my mouth and glug an entire cup of juice in one go. I don't even care that my hands are filthy. Lord Bearon stares at me the entire time.

"Is this a kink of yours?" I ask with a mouthful. "Watching women eat?"

He considers me and seems to be holding back a smirk. "I've never seen a woman like you eat like this before. Maybe it is."

I turn to him. "You don't know what kind of woman I am."

"I might know more than you think," he says, raising an eyebrow.

There's something cocky behind his eyes that irritates me, as does his self-assured air. I glare at him challengingly before piling scrambled eggs onto a fork.

"You are fiercely stubborn," Lord Bearon says. "I can tell that much. And proud." His dark eyes bore into me. "You don't trust easily, but I bet that when you do let your guard down, you love boldly and unapologetically, with all your heart. I can see you're very scared, despite the confidence in the way you to me. And I know that confidence is a mask for how uncertain you are."

I stare at him, unable to hide how stunned I am. No one has ever spoken to me like that before. Or seen through me like he just did. My voice is low when I ask, "What am I uncertain about?"

"About who you really are." He holds his gaze on me for a long moment.

I force myself to speak, not wanting him to see how much he's rattled me. "Not bad. You're observant, I'll give you that, but also very incorrect. My fiancé knows me better than anyone else. Far better than your generic, broad observations."

Lord Bearon tilts his head slightly. "Fiancé?"

"He is a great and powerful man," I say with my chin high. "A better man than you'll ever be. He will come looking for me, and he'll bring the six hells with him."

"Is that so?" Lord Bearon says, leaning forward. "By the time your fiancé figures out where you are and comes for you, I will likely have become fed up with your attitude and will gladly give you back."

I glower at him. That makes him chuckle, which annoys me even more. I can't help but notice, however, how full and pouty his lips are beneath his neatly trimmed beard.

I focus on the food as I don't feel comfortable looking at him for too long. The cinnamon scroll is less spiced than I'm used to, mostly consisting of dough, and it's clearly stale. The fruit is not fresh, but passable. The eggs have an odd aftertaste and the sausages are hot, but they're not as meaty as the ones in the Kingdom. I'm grateful for it all, though, after being so starved.

I don't tell Lord Bearon my opinions on the food, as while it would delight me to cut him down a peg or two, I've been raised never to insult a host. *Not a host, Clio. He's a damned captor.*

When I gulp down the coffee from one of the small cups, I burn my mouth and spill some on the table.

"Do they serve coffee cold from where you're from?" he asks with a smirk.

I give him another glare.

After a moment of quiet eating, I give him a sideways look. "Your guards called you a lord. Just what are you a lord of?"

"It is merely a title of respect," he says. "I'm sure it's the same for you and yours in the Kingdom?"

I shrug. "We have many titles for many people. They all serve a purpose, however."

He nods but says nothing and passes the time by sipping his coffee. Then he sits up straighter and clears his throat.

"I have to apologize for how you've been treated so far. I don't want you to be a prisoner here. I should never have put you in that cell. But, don't worry, you won't have to go back there. I want you to enjoy your breakfast, and your scalding hot coffee, and then I will have my people take you to your own rooms. You can bathe, and there will be clean clothes for you. If none suit your tastes, well, then... I'll have to see about finding more for you. You may request any items you need to make your stay more comfortable. I can't promise we'll have all the fancy luxuries you're used to in your kingdom, living in the royal castle and all, but I'll do what I can for you."

I swallow a mouthful of fruit and try not to show my shock. "Why would you be so nice to me?"

"I feel bad, is the truth. For not being able to take you home. So, while you're—"

"Wait. Why can't you take me home? If you feel so bad, just give me a horse and I'll be on my way. I won't tell anyone where I've been. I'll say I got lost while trying to flee the city and then fell and was knocked unconscious for a few days. I'll make something up. You and I can forget this ever happened."

He frowns, his beard shifting. His eyes are so dark and sorrowful. Or maybe that's just what he wants me to think. Now he's leaning forward on his elbows, his enormous arms are on full display. It's as though he has melons stuffed in his sleeves, the thick fabric straining to keep them hidden. His hands look more than twice the size of mine, and the veins beneath his skin course with power. I am reminded of his earlier threat, and how a single twitch of those massive hands could crush me.

"I wish it were so simple," he says. "I'm afraid you're with us for now. Until I can figure out what to do with you."

"Just send me on my way," I say, my voice rising with emotion.

"My decision is final." His eyes now shining with what I take to be anger. He must be used to people agreeing to everything he says. "I can't let you leave. Not until I know what the Kingdom is thinking or planning. So, while you're here, I want you to feel safe and comfortable."

I grit my teeth and say, "Fine, then. As you wish."

I choose to say nothing more. It's clear he's made up his mind and yelling at him isn't going to change anything. If he wants me to be a docile, submissive prisoner for him, then that's what I'll be for now. I'll be whatever he thinks I am. That way, he won't see what I'm really up to.

I pause when I catch something troubled in his eyes. Something deeply withdrawn. Like he's no longer in the room. He almost looks... lost. And sad. His face has completely changed. He catches me looking and snaps out of whatever thoughts had held him.

Lord Bearon moves to stand and pauses halfway up. He points to a sausage.

"What do you call them in the Kingdom?"

"That's... a sausage."

He smiles. "We call them that, too."

I'm perplexed as he stands and finishes the last of his coffee. There's a whimsical side to him I haven't noticed before. But he still has that smug arrogance, like he's pleased with himself.

"I will never trust you," I tell him. "And I will never thank you. For anything. I want you to know that."

He pauses and stares at me with an unreadable expression.

"I know exactly what situation I'm in," I continue, "and you can't make me see otherwise with any amount of food or baths or clothes or reassuring words. I am a Kingdom citizen being kept as a prisoner in the Oathlands. If a rabbit is green, you call it a green rabbit. You can pretend I am a guest, but I know what I really am. A prisoner."

"You have the wrong impression of the Oathlanders. I promise you we're not as bad as you've been raised to believe."

"Says the man holding me captive. Tell me, who was it that started the last war?"

His face hardens. "We did. But it wasn't for the reasons you think."

"I'm sure you see things differently from your side. And don't tell me what I think."

Lord Bearon strides around the table, his eyes searing through me. I force my body not to flinch as he takes a step in my direction, the air thick with tension.

"Do you know who Lady Moira is?" Something in his tone tells me he's gravely serious.

"I've never heard of her."

"That is part of your problem."

I hold my eyes on him, not backing down. My look hopefully tells him that he won't change how I think and feel.

"I can see you're growing annoyed with me," he says after a silence between us. "I don't want to... yell at you again. I apologize for that, by the way. I will leave you now, and when you're ready, they can escort you out." He turns to leave, but pauses. "By the way, *Wendy Allspice*..." He leans forward and sniffs. "You should bathe. You smell."

With that, he turns and strides to the double doors, his boots clopping on the hard floor.

While Lord Bearon speaks to his guards across the room with his back to me, I reach with my fingers and tuck the knife into my sleeve.

I will be getting out of here one way or another.

Chapter Eight

CLIO

The guards escort me to what they call my guest rooms. My interactions with Lord Bearon rumble through my mind and I can't get that damned man out of my thoughts. I know I can't trust him, and yet there have been glimpses of something gentle and kind behind his gruff exterior. Or, that's just what he wants me to think, at least.

There are three good-sized rooms with high ceilings, connected by sliding doors. The middle room is long, like a wide corridor, and looks to be for lounging and hosting, with large sofas and armchairs around soft carpets and a glass table. Square rooms are on either side, one for sleeping and one for dining. This isn't at all what I'd been expecting, and compared to my dungeon cell I feel like I'm practically walking through the Heavenly Halls.

What is most odd is how familiar the rooms' layout and design are. It almost feels like I'm in a warped version of the Royal Palace in the Kingdom, but without its modern tastes and far less polished. The color schemes of the rooms are mostly browns, maroons, and faded blacks that look gray, with some silver thrown in. Like a rustic, older version of the luxuries I'm used to.

"Is everything to your satisfaction, my lady?" One guard asks.

I turn to where he's standing with his hands clasped behind his back, beside the second guard. "Yes, thank you."

"Is there anything we can get for you? Anything you need?" the first guard asks.

I ponder that and shake my head. "What is it you do here?"

They stare at me blankly.

"Are you... servants? Guards? Soldiers?"

The second man says, "We serve Lord Bearon, ma'am." He has an accent from the Southern Isles, or perhaps Koprus.

I don't think I'll get anything more out of them, so I dismiss them as though they're my palace servants, before I recall where I am and who I am supposed to be.

Finally alone, I let out a long breath, feeling my shoulders drop. I wander casually around the middle room, becoming accustomed to my surroundings. There's a large window above a desk with pedestals on either side and a high-backed chair.

Out the window, I can see rocky cliff faces, trees and shrubs, and beyond that are a few buildings on the edge of the town. There isn't much of a view. This must be the back side of the tower that doesn't face the main town. I'll have to wait to get a good view of the Oathlands proper. The afternoon sky is overcast and gloomy, which matches how I feel.

The trees are massive here. I must be on the fourth or fifth floor, perhaps the sixth, and there are some trees on the ground that reach beyond my level. They look thick and sturdy, like they could hold small houses if some were built in them.

Below, I can just make out a courtyard and some gardens, but it's hard to see. There seems to be a wide perimeter of gardens around the entire tower.

I head into the bedroom and, once I feel I'm truly alone and unseen, I withdraw the hidden knife from my sleeve. I cut a line into the side of the mattress and tuck the knife inside, thinking of ways I can use it later.

"Right. Time to clean up," I mutter to myself. The thought of a bath actually gets me excited. I feel like burning my filthy clothes, even if they're my only link to home.

The bathroom is connected to the bedroom, and is surprisingly large, with a bathtub in the center as the main attraction. It is an old, classic bathtub with curved legs, adorned with gold engravings around the rim. I'm surprised to see something of such high quality. My first thought is that they stole this from the Kingdom at some point, but I dismiss it as a silly thought.

I remove my clothes and use the bath to shower first, pulling the curtain rail to give myself privacy despite being alone. I want to remove most of the grime and dirt before my bath. I've never been so filthy before.

When I finally climb into the drawn bathtub, I rejoice in the hot water and the floral scented soap bubbles I added. Some of my scrapes sting in the hot water, but it feels like a dream come true. I can't relax completely, not knowing if Lord Bearon has hidden spy holes anywhere.

Perhaps he or his guards are watching me bathe. Maybe he's out there now, plotting to kill me. I don't know what's going to happen in the next hour, let alone the next day and beyond. But for now, I try to enjoy my glorious bath.

I can't get Lord Bearon out of my head. That calculated way he speaks, the way he watches me, as if he sees everything I am and am not all at once. Those dark eyes, refusing to look away from mine first, the tilt of his lips...

My fingers began to drift down my abdomen without me realizing it, and I quickly pull them back, scolding myself for the heat in my blood as I imagine this strange, wicked man standing before me.

But after everything, I could use a little... relaxation, couldn't I? I rarely had time to myself in the castle, and I certainly have it now. Besides, it's been a while since my body has felt like this, especially since I had seen so little of my fiance lately. It's only natural that, after so much time without such a release, my body might be desperate for such a thing, easy to rile up. Especially since all it seems to take is a handsome face and a little bit of attention to get me all bothered.

I groan a little to myself and try to shake the image of Lord Bearon out of my mind, hoping to pull Leonas' to the forefront instead. But it's been a long while since I've seen him, and with everything that's happened, it seems my mind doesn't really want to focus on the sweet memories of the past.

Lord Bearon laughs in my mind. *Tell yourself that all you'd like, Allspice. But don't pretend your fingers aren't moving lower with each word I speak.*

I hate that he's right—even if he is just a figment of my imagination. And I hate that I'm not at all inclined to stop those fingers again. No, I deserve a little release, don't I? *Something* to quell my nerves, even if just for a moment?

A shaky breath leaves my lips as my fingers brush against my folds, and I slide them against the growing slickness. My head tips back and my mouth falls open as my fingers move upward and find that sensitive bud.

I circle my fingers around it, unable to bite back the moan or stop my hips from pushing down, from rolling with the friction to create more of it. Lord Bearon watches me from behind my eyelids, the figment I've created of him grinning, nodding with satisfaction. *Yes,* he says. *Show me how you like it.*

I start to move faster, and my other hand slides down, too. I nudge a finger at my entrance and stretch it slowly with circles that slowly grow wider and wider until I sink a finger inside of myself and hook it in as deep as I can. My hands and my hips are moving in sync, creating a rhythm that has me gasping, unable to control myself or the sounds that leave me. The water in the tub begins to form waves as I become wilder, drawing closer to the climax that builds at the base of my spine.

I slide another finger inside myself and push it in as deep as I can until it meets that most sensitive spot inside of me, and my hips grind down as my inner walls clench around my two fingers. I scissor them inside myself, imagining that Lord Bearon is striding closer now, hoping to get a better look at what I'm doing, as if he wishes to memorize every last one of my movements.

Lord Bearon says, *You're about to come, aren't you?*

I'm nodding, as if he's really here, and I cry out as my walls clench against my scissored fingers.

Go on then, he tells me, just as my fingers dip against my g-spot once more, and I pinch my clit with my other hand.

My hips rock as I orgasm and a long, low moan leaves my lips as water splashes from the tub until I finally still, and it calms little by little. My breathing relaxes as my imaginary Lord Bearon crosses his arms and smirks at me, pleased that I listened to him.

I bat the mental image away and scowl as I open my eyes, immediately annoyed with myself for... all of that. Now that I've already gotten myself off, I'm far less quick to excuse the action. How horrible am I to imagine a man other than my fiance while pleasuring myself?

Oh, my gods. And what if someone really was spying on me? At least I never said anything out loud.

I let myself linger in the shame for only a moment longer before shaking myself out of it. I can't let myself relish in useless feelings—I need to think about things beyond myself.

My only hope is that my Kingdom people are on their way to retrieve me at any moment. Well, hopefully sometime after my bath.

My mind wanders to the last time I'd had a bath. I'd been with my fiancé, Leonas. I miss his kind eyes, and how he'd look at me full of love and adoration. I can picture the tufts of hair on his chest, mixed with the soapy bubbles of the bath, and can practically smell the rose and lavender from that time.

A sudden wave of worry washes over me as I consider the thought that in my memories I don't recall feeling the same way. My stomach turns, but before I have a chance to take the thought any further, I push it away with a strength of will, determined to not dwell on it.

I know Leonas will come for me. But that's if he can determine the attack came from the Oathlanders. Perhaps my father and Leonas are currently on their way to attack another land, thinking they are the culprits. I begin to worry that war is going to break out across the land while I'm kept prisoner here.

I start to get a headache from worrying and overthinking. I know I won't be able to fully enjoy this bath, but I make the most of it. Clearly.

I feel like a new person once I'm out and wrapped in a robe. It's an old and frail robe that smells of dust, but it'll do. The sun has begun to set and there is a reddish golden glow streaming in through the windows. It must be late afternoon, but it feels like the end of the day for me.

They have hung clothes up on a metal railing in the bedroom. I scrunch my face at the sight of them.

They are shabby, gaudy clothes for the most part, while some are just plain and horrendous. None suit modern tastes, or even any modern tailoring. Perhaps these are the height of fashion in the Oathlands. I try to decide which ones I can stand to wear, even though I have little choice in the matter. I'm surprised, however, to find that most are my size.

Does he just have a bunch of women's clothes lying around? I wonder. *Maybe these are the clothes of all the women he's brought to his tower and killed.* I shudder the thought away.

I choose a brown dress and a cream blouse with overly long, flowy sleeves. Not my taste, but they'll do.

My thoughts drift back to Lord Bearon. I can't help but think of his dark eyes, his pouty lips, and his deep voice. And how frustrating he is to talk to.

I know I can never truly trust him. His people have caused enough death and destruction to the Kingdom over the years for them to never be trusted. So I wonder why he's being so accommodating to me. He must be luring me into a false sense of safety to get information from me. I'm sure he has an agenda. All men do.

My throbbing head tells me how exhausted I am. It's been a long few days, and that bath has really relaxed my muscles. Once dressed, I lay down on the bed to close my eyes just…for… a moment.

Chapter Nine

CLIO

It's not until something wakes me up that I realize I've fallen asleep. A misty orange light is coming through the windows, telling me how late in the day it is. I must have been asleep for hours.

Two uniformed men are standing by the doorway of my bedroom. It takes me a second to realize one of them has just coughed to wake me up.

"Apologies, my lady," one of them says. "I'm here to tell you that Lord Bearon has requested your company."

I groggily lift my head, noting how wild and wayward my hair is. I nod to the guards and hesitate as I sit up. I refuse to let myself think of the things I've done to the thought of that man. It wasn't because of *him*. Not at all. It was more circumstance than anything. Still, I can't help the memories flashing through my brain, no matter how much I wish to tamp them down.

"Would you allow me a moment of privacy?"

"Of course." They nod curtly and step out into the main lounge area.

I spare a thought for the knife hidden in the mattress. Do I dare bring it out and risk them seeing me? What if they search me when we leave the room? I decide it's too risky to take the knife now, and I know too little about the town and my escape plan to make any moves.

I stand before the mirror on a dresser and consider brushing my out-of-control hair. I tell myself I don't need to look respectable for an audience with his Lord Smugness. Then I decide that some brushing won't hurt. A lady should always look respectable. Even, I guess, while in the hands of the enemy.

There are four different perfume bottles on the dresser, but I ignore those and make my way out to the guards, smoothing out my dress.

I walk with the two men through the corridors and down flights of stairs. While we walk along a wide hallway adorned with portraits of old people, I ask them, "May I know your names?"

The one nearest me has curly black hair and a boyish face, but faint lines across his brow make me guess his age to be mid-thirties, perhaps a good ten years older than me.

"My name is Forest, my lady. Forest Quill," he says. I recognize him as one of the men who had escorted me from my cell earlier.

The other man isn't familiar to me. He is taller and broader with blond hair and a stony expression. "Samuels, ma'am."

I get the impression Samuels doesn't like me very much, but at least Forest seems amiable enough.

"May I ask, what is it that Lord Bearon does?" I ask, watching carefully for their reactions.

Stoic Samuels says, "Lord Bearon is the keeper of the tower, ma'am."

"I see. But what does that mean? What does he... do?"

Samuel keeps his gaze ahead, and I guess that means he's done talking to me. Forest shares a small smile with me.

"Lord Bearon watches out for us all," Forest says. "He protects the tower and all people within the Oathlands' borders."

That gives me even more questions than answers, but I have a feeling I will not get much else from these two. At least they have some manners and a sense of respect. Not that they know I'm a princess. The 'ma'am' sounds a little odd; it's not common in the Kingdom, but I guess it's more popular out here.

They lead me to what looks like a back entrance of the tower. Beyond the wide open doorway, I can see shrubs and foliage and smell the fresh, floral scents of a garden.

Lord Bearon is standing outside, waiting for me. He is wearing a sharp white jacket with a black buttoned shirt, and black trousers with knee-high boots. The jacket is cut well to suit his large frame and accentuate his broad shoulders, and is longer in the back than the front. An odd style that I haven't often seen in the Kingdom.

The red sun is washing the sky in a vibrant golden red light, highlighting the clouds and shooting sun beams through them. On one side, the sky has already darkened to a deep blue.

"Would you care for a walk around the gardens?" He asks as I draw closer with the guards and his eyes momentarily roam over my chosen clothes. "I was thinking you might like to stretch your legs after being cooped up all afternoon."

He's holding two items wrapped in a tissue cloth. "I also thought you might be hungry. Seeing as you hardly ate breakfast." He has a twinkle in his eyes that makes him appear younger.

I take one of the wrapped parcels and see it is a kind of bread roll. Thick bread is tightly wrapped around a minced meat filling. It's warm and smells delicious. He must see from my expression that I'm unfamiliar with it.

"It is a *lofousa* roll. Otherwise known as a shepherd's roll."

"I don't think I've had one before," I say, studying it.

"Thick-sliced *fous* bread, wrapped around a mixture of meat and vegetables, with a gravy sauce. It is baked, and comes out crisp and heavenly."

"It sounds like the house cakes we make in the Kingdom," I say. "But those are smaller and rounder, without gravy. We call them cakes even though they're pies. They can be sweet or savory."

"Yes, these can be sweet too, with a bean paste or custard filling. You see, our people are more similar than you might think."

"Is this why you summoned me here? To show me this meat pie and reinforce the similarities between us?"

"Well, that, and it's a lovely afternoon. I usually like to walk around this golden time. And I'd like to show you my gardens. I'm quite proud of them, if I must say."

I nod, holding the meat roll with both hands and feeling its warmth. I take a careful bite as we begin strolling, leaving the two guards by the entrance.

The garden stretches out ahead and to our side, where tall hedges lead to other parts of the grounds. The base of the tower is on our other side, and when I look up I get a sense of vertigo as I see the far-off points of the top, fading into the dark sky. The tower is an unflattering off-black, with dark browns and some ashen grays accenting the towers and peaks.

It's my first good look at the structure, but from this location it's hard to get a good sense of its design. It looks very old, though. Like it's been trapped in time.

There are enormous hedge structures around the paved pathways, some cut into the shape of sea animals or wildlife, and a water fountain with an angelic figure in the center. Lord Bearon points out that the figure is their patron saint of fortune, Siv Faestia. He also explains that *Siv* is an old word for Lady.

I notice how nicer my captor is to me now, almost as though he's decided to try a different tact. Maybe he's trying to lure me into a false sense of safety. While we walk and talk, I keep a constant eye out for anything that looks out of place, or anything that could be coming for me. This may all be some kind of trap.

"What do you think of the *lofousa* roll?" he asks.

I nod, swallowing a bite. "It's lovely. Thank you. This... gravy sauce? It's very good. What is it?"

He eyes me sideways. "Butter and flour, for the most part. There are many variations."

I nod appreciatively. *Stop being so nice to him. You don't have to be polite.*

Lord Bearon straightens his posture. "Now, I want to reiterate a few things. I want you to understand that you are not a prisoner here. You are free to go about the tower and its grounds, but you are not permitted to leave the grounds. You have free rein throughout the entire tower. But I'm afraid there is an exception of my bedroom. That is out of bounds."

Why is he bringing up his bedroom? And why does it remind me of what I did in the bathtub? I turn to him. "I wasn't planning to go into your bedroom, anyway."

He nods in agreement, though doesn't meet my eyes. "I think you should make the most of your time here, even if you may feel trapped with no say in the matter."

"Maybe I feel that way because I am trapped with no say in the matter."

He frowns at that, gazing over the garden.

There's something conflicted in his eyes, his brows deeply creased. Has he planned something against me and is now having second thoughts? Or does he regret he has to betray my trust and have me killed? My heart has begun to race as we walk, my eyes darting all around without making it obvious that I'm on high alert.

"Tell me about yourself," he says after a silence, surprising me.

"Why do you care about your captive?"

He casually takes a bite of his roll. Chewing, he says, "Believe it or not, I'm genuinely interested in who you are as someone more than our *accidental* captive. It's not often we get a visitor from the Kingdom in these parts. Well, one that isn't spying, scouting, or swinging a sword."

"Nice alliteration," I mutter, then add, "I guess I'm the same as any other Kingdom folk. We bathe each morning in the blood of our enemies. Eat raw meat from livestock we kill. Chant and dance naked around burning incense to secure our city's safety. You know, the usual."

"I see," he says, nodding. "And this naked dancing? Is that something you will be performing during your stay here?"

My throat seizes.

He lets out a low chuckle at my expression. "I jest. But, honestly, I am curious about you. For instance, what are your dreams? Your aspirations?"

I eye him warily. I can't remember the last time anyone has asked me something like that. I can't recall even Leonas asking me such a question. I've always been so close with my father that he knows everything about me, so he's never had to ask me about my dreams, as he thinks he knows them all already.

I decide to take a chance and open up a little. What harm can it do?

"I've... always wanted to help people. I suppose that's been my calling in life. To see to the protection and comfort of my people, and those I care for. I want to make a difference in this life. I know it's silly to think that an entire city rests on my shoulders. But I just want everyone to be happy and feel safe. All that our previous generations have known is war and the brink of war. And the aftermath of death and destruction. Sometimes I think about having my own fields and crops to tend to. To feel like I am making a difference to give future generations life instead of death."

"You want to make a difference to your Kingdom," Lord Bearon says thoughtfully. "I understand your desire. I share it. For my people."

We reach a white stone bench and he gestures for us to sit. I'm happy to sit and be able to focus on the meat roll more. The more I eat of it, the more I realize how famished I've been. I take it as a sign that my body needs sustenance and I've always been a believer in listening to our bodies.

The scent of warm spices comes to me when a breeze blows over us. His scent has an interesting kick to it, with deeper hints of vanilla and citrus. It is strangely familiar, I feel, though for the life of me I am not able to place it.

As if he can sense my desire to eat, Lord Bearon doesn't ask questions and allows me to eat for a while. I can't help but look behind me at times to see if anyone is approaching, wondering if he has me facing this direction for a reason.

"You are perfectly safe here," he says. "I give you my word. If I wanted you dead, you would be already, and it would've been by my own hand. I promise, Wendy Allspice, you are safe."

That is only mildly reassuring, but I sigh and wrestle internally for a moment before saying, "My name is not Wendy."

"I know. I guessed that saying the name would prompt you to tell me your real name."

The honesty in his words takes me aback. I appreciate it.

I consider saying my name, but decide to ask some questions of my own. "You mentioned you had some business today?" I take a large bite of the roll to indicate that I want him to talk for a while. The hot smoky gravy tastes so good mixed with the meat and vegetables.

"It's been... a hard day," Lord Bearon says, sounding exhausted. "I... made some difficult visits to people today. I went to the homes of the men who had died in your Kingdom, and explained to them their loved ones are no longer with us because of my inability to keep them safe. Because of my foolishness."

I'm struck again by his honesty, and the deep sorrow in his low voice. I can't imagine having to go through what he went through today. He could have had others break the news, or throw the blame onto the Kingdom, but it sounds like he took full responsibility for those deaths. I wonder how many other men would do the same.

"They were under my care," Lord Bearon continues, as if talking to himself. "And they were killed because of my foolish and reckless actions. I convinced fifty of our soldiers to ride with me to the Kingdom, telling them that our town will perish unless we do something."

"And that *something* was stealing our gold?"

He shakes his head and stares off into the distance, that conflicted look hardening his face. "The reason for my actions means little in the grand scheme of things. What's done is done, and there were unnecessary deaths on both sides. And that is on me alone."

"Those men chose to follow you," I say, not sure why I'm trying to comfort him. "It must have been very difficult to speak to their families."

"Everyone must own up to their actions, and always speak up, no matter how difficult it is to get the words out." His voice has fallen to a gravelly whisper. "Too many people pass the blame or make up excuses for this or that. But a true man owns up to his mistakes and has to live with them. Every day."

I'm left staring at him, not knowing what to say. I didn't think he'd be able to impress me as much as he just has. Is this really the same man who'd threatened to tear my head off if I tried to escape?

It's just words, I tell myself. *Don't believe the words. Look at the actions.* A true man would not keep a woman captive against her will.

"Enough about me," he says, clearing his throat. "How about you? What's a difficult thing you've had to do lately?"

I frown at the question. The first thing that comes to mind was when I'd been told I'd have to marry a man I'd never met before. I hated the idea of an arranged marriage. One made for political reasons above anything else. But, once I'd met Leonas and had gotten to know him, I had fallen for him, and so had ended up happy to be betrothed.

That's not something I'm willing to share with my captor, however. Especially since lower-born people aren't often thrown into arranged marriages. "Well, as the daughter of a cook, difficult decisions rarely come my way."

"You are lucky," he says, looking into the distance with a forlorn expression, his dark eyes like a storm at sea.

Then he seems to snap out of that and looks at me, almost amused. "A woman named Wendy whose real name is not Wendy. A cook's daughter who doesn't know how to make gravy."

His questions go unspoken, but they're clear on his face. I notice how there is some green and hazel in his eyes when they're highlighted in the sun. I can't seem to look away.

"My name is Clio," I tell him, feeling conflicted about revealing my name. "Clio Welling. My mother is Kara Welling, one of the cooks in the royal palace, and my father was a sheepherder who passed away a long time ago." At least I gave the real name of one of our cooks. My father always taught me to lie with a sprinkle of the truth. "Is that enough for you?"

There is no way I'm going to reveal my true identity to this man. If he knew he had the niece of the King in his possession, there's no telling what he might do to me. Threaten my life to get what he wants? Kill me to send a message to the Kingdom?

"Thank you for telling me the truth, Clio." My name sounds odd on his lips, like he's had to force it out, but it isn't a terrible sound. "It is nice to meet you."

I smile and shyly look away. I'll play nice for now, if that's what he wants. But I've already started to form a plan of escape. In a day or two, I'll be out of here. Once I'm in the town, I'll pass as one of the Oathlanders in their clothes. Then I'll just need to get a horse and I'll be on my way. I want to ask Lord Bearon if he tends to any horses, but I'm afraid the question would give my intentions away. For now, I'll wait and devise my plan.

Another awkward silence comes over us. One that feels burdened with unspoken words. So I finish the rest of my meat roll. The gravy has soaked into the bottom and moistened the bread. The last few messy bites are my favorite, despite bits of filling falling away and some gravy dripping onto my hands. I quickly dab my face and hands with the paper that had been wrapped around my roll.

Lord Bearon hands me the paper wrapped around his own half-eaten roll. "The last bites can be messy."

I gratefully take the paper and wipe my hands and face some more, feeling very unlady-like in the moment. I'm not used to eating with my hands. When I meet his eyes, I decide to voice that.

"I'm not used to eating with my hands so much."

"Well, we'll have to rectify that. Some of the best foods are eaten with your hands. Like spice boats. You know those crispy wheat bowls with the spiced mix in them? You can eat the bowl while you eat the mix. The smaller ones are spice cups."

"We have the spice boats," I tell him. "But they're fairly mild. And we eat them with utensils on a plate."

His eyes widen. "Sacrilege."

Something about the way he said that makes me laugh, and we share a smile. Our eyes lock onto each other and I wonder what's caught his eye so much. Then he tentatively reaches out to bring a hand up to my face.

I'm frozen with uncertainty as he brushes a thumb over my cheek, by the corner of my mouth. It's a slow, gentle brush that catches me off guard. A gravy-soaked crumb falls away.

"You just had a... bit of..." he says, but stumbles over his words and isn't able to finish his sentence.

I look away, feeling my face flush. "Yes. Thank you."

I can no longer meet his eyes after that oddly tender moment. But I can feel him staring at me. I wish I could turn to see what is going on behind his eyes.

Footsteps approach, startling us both.

A uniformed guard comes to a stiff stop, hands clasped behind him. "My Lord. The General Commander requests a moment with you. He is waiting for you in the welcome hall."

Lord Bearon stands up. "Thank you, Amos. Could you please escort Lady Welling to her rooms?"

The guard nods briskly.

Lord Bearon turns to me as I get up. "It's getting late. While you're free to do as you wish within the ground, I suggest you call it a night for today. And, just so you know–wherever you go, my guards will be with you. But I have instructed them not to get in your way or make their presence smothering."

I nod, not knowing what else to say about my situation. I'm clearly a prisoner, but I don't want to get into the semantics of the matter again.

Lord Bearon leaves through the misty haze that has fallen over the gardens. I hadn't realized how dark it had gotten around us. The deep blue sky has remnants of red, slowly fading. The first stars have started to twinkle in the gloom.

I allow myself to be escorted away and have to wonder what Lord Bearon had been hiding in those last moments. Had he not wanted me to be seen by this General Commander? Is his meeting with the General Commander a secret, or something to do with me?

I can't help but feel, despite his insistence of being open and honest with me, that Lord Bearon is keeping a lot from me.

Chapter Ten
CLIO

I'm unable to relax. While I've always felt better in my own company than that of others, I can't help but at least consider the idea of exploring the tower and seeing what information I can get out of the guards or anyone else I come across. Perhaps a maid or serving woman, if they have those here. But it's getting late and I'm still weary from the past few days, a dull ache remaining in the back of my head.

I decide to stay in my rooms, but explore what I can. In the square dining room, my eyes land on a large portrait of a dark-haired woman. She has stern green eyes and sharp cheekbones. Perhaps this is Lord Bearon's wife. Maybe a late wife. Or possibly his mother? There could be some similarities in their tilted brows. There is no inscription or plaque to tell me her identity.

While I stroll, I come to the open window and can hear faint singing somewhere outside. Coming from the town? The wind carries the sound, so it's hard to determine the words, but it's a jovial song with many voices. The starry night sky feels alive and full of wonder, reminding me of the nights spent outside while on the way to the Oathlands. Back when Lord Bearon had pointed out a few constellations to me.

I have to wonder what kind of savages sing songs like this. However, even though I haven't been to the town, I'm already starting to see how civilized these Oathlanders are. They're not as wild and savage as some in the Kingdom believe them to be, though it pains me to admit it, to admit that my kingdom was wrong.

Though I might begrudgingly consider these people civil and good, there is no denying the... shaky history of our kingdoms. Hundreds of years ago, the Kingdom of Aer and the Oathlands had been on good terms. But the Oathlands had invaded. They had cast the first stone. And for centuries, the wars raged on. There had never been a period of peace that lasted over twenty years.

The previous war, known as the Last Blood War, was over twenty years ago and is considered the last great war between the kingdoms. After the devastation left behind by the First and the Second Blood Wars, not to mention countless battles, there had been a sort of silent agreement between our people. It seemed that no one wanted any more death and destruction for the sake of old wounds and revenge. For two decades now, we've lived in a state of frozen truce, though neither side has called it that. Or called it anything.

Many say that the wars are finally over, although there are those who know history better and believe another war is inevitable. A final war. One that will wipe out one of the kingdoms for good. But then, people have been saying that since before I was born.

The only road to peace is for one kingdom to disappear, my father always told me.

I make my way to the bed and, sure that I'm alone, bring out the knife hidden in the side of the mattress. I'm relieved to see it is still there.

It's a simple bread knife with some serrations, but it should be enough to cause damage. I've never hurt anyone before, but I think I can do it if I truly need to. If it means my freedom and safety.

I tuck the knife back through the slit in the mattress when the feeling of being watched comes over me. I'm alone in the rooms, however, so it's an odd feeling and I dismiss it.

It is evenings like this that I miss the comfort of my Leonas. No doubt he is a wreck, knowing I'm out there somewhere, waiting for his rescue. I hope my father is coping with me being gone. He's still fairly young for his mid-fifties, but I've noticed how he's been slowing down these past few years; how tired he gets at times.

And yet, despite my worries of my fiancé and father, I find myself thinking of Lord Bearon's tender thumb on my cheek, and his startlingly deep, troubled eyes. I'm almost certain he's trying to trick me into letting my guard down, but that moment between us felt startlingly honest. Like it was the first time I was seeing him.

And I hate how easy he is to talk to. How easy it is to speak freely with him. I suppose I'm too used to having to watch what I say in the royal palace, and keeping up with the standards my father expects of me. I am too free in the role I'm playing as an ordinary girl.

I know I will never fully trust an Oathlander, but then why do I feel so comfortable in the presence of one? *Because he's playing with you, foolish woman.*

It makes me wonder why Leonas or my father never asked me about my aspirations and desires. Why they've never sought to know what I truly think and feel. Because they think they know me already? And maybe they do. Maybe they know me better than I think and do not need to ask those sorts of questions.

My mind feels numb and throbs with exhaustion from all the back-and-forth thoughts. I decide to call it a night. By this time I would normally already be in my nightgown, winding down the last hours of the day with a book and tea. But I've felt the need to remain fully dressed in this strange new place.

As I look over the nightgowns hanging in a wardrobe, I feel a chill coming through the open window. Each room has a single window facing the back of the tower. The other two are closed but my bedroom one remains open as I've never enjoyed sleeping in a hot room.

I consider closing the window and then pause when I look outside. Within the dark shapes of the shifting trees, there is a large shape on one of the branches. A tall, rounded shape like a beast sitting on its haunches. It's completely black save for a pair of glowing red eyes, which are looking directly at me.

The sight of the great beast chills my blood and steals my breath. For a frightening moment, I simply stare into the depths of those blood-red eyes, seemingly hovering in the darkness. I've never seen anything like it.

My eyes dart back around the room while I try to remain still, not wanting to make any quick actions. Can I get to the knife before the thing leaps into the room? I doubt the little blade would do anything against it, anyway. Maybe I can call for help. The guards are probably close to my rooms.

My heart is racing when I look back at the beast. But it's no longer there. It takes me a few seconds to adjust to the darkness out the window to be sure it isn't there anymore. As if instantly vanished, the beast is gone. My heart still pounds.

Was there even anything out there, or had it been my paranoid mind playing tricks on me?

I shiver as I make my way to the window, expecting something to jump out at me at any moment. I close the shutters and the curtains, feeling somewhat safer with the barrier between me and the outside. Another violent shiver shakes my shoulders.

I climb into the bed, above the side with the knife, and listen out for potential threats, hearing all the bumps and creaks in the quiet tower, until sleep eventually takes me.

Chapter Eleven
Arthur

I find my brother in the lounge, helping himself to a drink from the corner bar. The golden hues of the brightly lit room feel jarring coming from the growing darkness in the gardens.

From Rourk's hardened features, I can tell he's troubled. And pissed off.

"We have bad news and bad news," Rourk says, not looking up from the two glasses of whiskey he's pouring.

"I'll take the bad news first," I sigh, feeling the weariness of the day creeping through me.

"Our spies have indicated there is movement from the Kingdom. They may be preparing an attack."

"An attack on us?"

"We're not sure yet. It's possible they believe the bandits who attacked them were from the Oathlands. We are the likeliest culprits. But we have to wait and see for now. And be ready."

I rest against a side table as a dizzy spell hits me. Bile builds in my throat, threatening vomit. "Hells, I have doomed us all."

Rourk slams the bottle down on the counter a little too hard. "We have yet to determine if that is the case. It could be that there is no attack. Perhaps they are fortifying their defenses or preparing for a possible attack they may never launch."

"What can I do to help?" I ask.

Rourk chuckles mirthlessly, coming over to hand me a glass. "For now, you do nothing more. You've done enough." He sips his drink and watches me closely. "One of your men said you had company?"

I don't let myself look away from his gaze, don't let him doubt me for a moment. "Just a bed maid," I say casually. "Not exactly a Lord or Lady." *Not exactly a captive, either.*

Rourk has something else on his mind. I can tell from how he's unable to look at me for too long. His long hair is a little disheveled, flaring out around the ears, which tells me he's been nervously running his hands through his hair.

"What is it?" I have to ask.

He paces and turns to me. "Captain Angus Tryphon was part of the company that went with you to the Kingdom, correct?"

I swallow through a dry throat. "Yes—he was slain during the chaos. I spoke with his family this afternoon."

"You spoke to his wife?"

"I did. Why do you ask?"

"Captain Tryphon's daughter, Tabetha, has gone missing."

I raise my brows. "Missing? Kidnapped?"

"We don't know yet," Rourk says, going back to pacing. "The little girl has been prone to wandering off and getting herself lost. But her mother says she hasn't been seen for days. Since around the time you would have snuck away with your platoon."

I frown in thought, feeling a chill wash over me. "I will have my men keep an eye out for Tabetha. I can send scouts around the city tonight. I... her mother didn't say anything when I spoke to her earlier."

Rourk nods. "They don't want to worry people, in case the girl finds her way back home. These days, it doesn't take much to spook the town and have whispers of an attack or kidnapping spreading like wildfire. And after your trip to the Kingdom... we don't want those kinds of rumors spreading. That's how wars are started, you know." The joke falls flat on his tongue.

I sip my whiskey, rejoicing in the fiery liquid going down. I'll probably have another glass once Rourk leaves.

He's watching me carefully again. "How is May?"

"She's fine. I haven't seen her since yesterday, but you know how she is. She's like a cat who goes about her own business."

"I know," Rourk says solemnly. He pauses for a moment in thought before finishing the last of his whiskey. "As for this possible Kingdom attack, I will know more in the morning. It's too early to make any judgements just yet. And if their army does leave the city, it could be they head elsewhere. Perhaps to Koprus in the south. They've had their share of bad blood."

"Except that was ancient history. Koprus and Aer have been on good terms for over a century. Their trade routes are stronger than ever."

Rourk's glass clinks on the counter when he puts it down. "Blood never forgets."

It pains me to see him so troubled and distracted. "How did it go with the Grandmaster General today?"

Rourk shakes his head, and I can see in his eyes that he's contemplating another drink as well. "He was not happy, as was to be expected. He demanded to court-martial you, but I managed to convince him otherwise."

"How did you manage that?"

"I said that you were more valuable to us all if left to your own devices, without being shackled. I lied, of course."

A mirthless chuckle escapes me. "You're a good brother."

"I'm a fool. And so are you. That's how we got ourselves in this situation. I'm meant to be second-in-command of our military and fifty of my soldiers run away with you in the middle of the night, after what I'm sure was a rousing speech on your part. Now we have a military force that's three times as large as our own, potentially amassing to attack us. If another war happens, Arthur, we might not walk away from it."

"We will do whatever we must," I say. "Whatever has to be done. Our people are stronger than ever. Together, we can make a difference and protect ourselves. I know it."

"Is that from one of your speeches that the people love so much?" Rourk asks, and I can hear the slight humor in his tone. "I swear, I still don't know why they love you so much. Like you're their guardian angel or patron saint."

"I've only ever tried to do what's best for our people," I retort, thinking of what ruin I've brought to us. "Though perhaps it's best that I just stay away from them."

There's something dark and serious behind Rourk's eyes. "You listen to me, brother. You're not an animal that needs to be caged. You know who you are. The people know who you are. It isn't such a stretch for you to live up to their praise."

I nod, turning away from his gaze. It's moments like this that I have to wonder who I really am, deep inside. There are far too many sides to factor in. What would Clio think of me if she knew the real me? And, more importantly, why do I care what she thinks?

It's hard to ignore that she's been on my mind ever since we found her stowed away in our wagon.

I suggest a second drink each, but Rourk says he has to head back. It's been a very long day for both of us.

Once I see my brother out, my thoughts shift back to Clio, several floors above me, likely sleeping by now. Should I do the right thing and just let her leave? Or is executing her and denying she was ever here the best thing to do for our people? Neither option sounds particularly appealing to me.

Maybe I just want to keep her for myself. Even if she can be infuriatingly annoying. There aren't many people willing to talk to me the way she does. It's amusing, in its own way.

Mesmerizing.

Chapter Twelve

CLIO

The next morning brings with it a new resolve. I wake up determined to find a way out of the Oathlands, away from the clutches of my captor. I intend to see as much as I can and *learn* as much as I can, in order to devise a plan of escape. I will not be a docile guest pandering to the whim of my abductor.

I feel remarkably better after a night of sleep, and the dull pounding in my head has mostly gone. I only feel it when I bend down or turn too quickly.

I choose a green wrap-around dress with a faint floral print. It has an asymmetrical closing with one side wrapped around the other, tied at the front opening. It's a little like some of the dresses I would normally wear, but about fifty years out of fashion.

Before I leave, I take out the knife from within the mattress and tuck it into my dress. It fits snug against my hip. I'll have to be careful about how I move or bend. I feel better having the knife on me, especially with the thought of that great beast lurking in the darkness last night. If it had been real, that is, and not just in my mind.

When I leave my room, I see there is one guard stationed outside. He nods respectfully but does not say anything.

"I suppose you'll be following me wherever I go?" I ask him.

He nods again. "That is correct."

I should have known that I would not truly be trusted on my own.

Like the others I've seen, this guard is fairly young. So far, all the guards here have been around early to late twenties, with a few older exceptions. I suppose they keep them while they're in their prime and discard them the year they've passed. No weak links, even if it means a smaller army. For that, I suspect they might have a stronger chain. But how far can it stretch?

In the open door of one room, I see a chambermaid dusting and cleaning. Down a corridor, I pass a large woman with a chef's apron, who smiles warmly at me. The tower is busier during the day than I'd expected.

At times I'd see another guard who would watch me closely, but none ever make their presence known and always keep their distance. I now have two regular guards who slowly keep up with my wandering.

I notice one of my regular followers is that friendly young man with the curly black hair I'd met yesterday. He reminds me his name is Forest and wishes me a good day. I wonder if the guards have been instructed not to engage in conversation with me.

I also wonder if I'll run into Lord Bearon, or if he'll call for me. Then I tell myself I shouldn't care if I see him today or not. I shouldn't be thinking about him as much as I have been.

Down one hallway, I come across a row of portraits. They're all of older people who are wearing regal attire, almost like royalty but without the golden adornments.

I stop by one painting which is familiar. The woman staring out into the distance is the same woman depicted in my rooms. The one with the startling green eyes and striking cheekbones. She is a decade or so older in this painting but still has her sharp, serious features, with her hair up in a tight bun. Her shimmering green scaled dress matches her eyes. I believe I have a similar dress, but mine is off the shoulder.

The plaque above the portrait reads *Lady Moira Alacante*.

Where have I heard that name before? Then I remember that yesterday, Lord Bearon asked me if I knew of a Lady Moira. This must be the woman he meant.

Is she his wife? Or a deceased wife? Her second name is not familiar to me either, though that's hardly a surprise, considering how little I know of these people.

I continue wandering for a while and go down a winding staircase to a lower level. The area opens up by the staircase to show five floors down to the ground level, to where I believe is the entrance lobby of the tower. I head down the corridor of this next level and check the first door I find.

I peek into what looks like an enormous library with two levels. The high ceiling has a small glass dome that lets in a ray of sunlight into the center of the room.

Ahead are rows of tables, and all around the sides in concentric circles are shelving units of books. There must be thousands of books.

I startle when I see I'm not alone. There is a young girl sitting at one table, hunched over a book. She must be in her mid-teens, at least. Her long dark hair hides some of her pale face from view, but when she looks up at me, I see cool blue eyes staring back. There is a wisdom in them that sparks, but there's a caution that lies underneath it.

The girl frowns at me. "Are you lost?"

"I'm just... exploring," I say. I hadn't expected to find a young girl in the tower. My first guess is that this is Lord Bearon's daughter. I hadn't even thought of him as a father.

"Exploring?" the girl says, clearly confused. "Who are you?"

I pause a moment, wondering what to say. "My name is Clio. I am a... guest of Lord Bearon."

The girl scrutinizes me. I can tell she doesn't believe me, but she nods as though she's lost interest in who I am.

I take a few steps closer. "What are you reading?"

She holds up the heavy hardback book. "The history of Aeros."

I raise an eyebrow. "The history of the continent?"

She shrugs. "It covers the various ruling kingdoms over the years. Did you know that once, the primary language of the world was Koprian?"

I can't help but be surprised. Wise, indeed. "I did, actually. I must admit, I don't think I've ever seen someone your age reading a historical book."

"I'm interested in knowledge," she says, shrugging again.

"Can I ask your name?"

She looks up at me. "May."

I have to have an answer to my burning question. "It's nice to meet you, May. I didn't know Lord Bearon had a daughter."

She opens her mouth to say something, but we're interrupted by a presence in the doorway. I expect to see a guard, but I straighten when I see Lord Bearon is there.

"Apologies for the interruption," he says. He summons me over with his eyes. I wonder why he doesn't just ask me to come over to him.

I excuse myself, telling May it was nice to meet her, and head out into the corridor with Lord Bearon.

"Good morning," he says with a smile that feels equal parts genuine and forced. "I am about to go into town, and I thought you might like to join me."

"Oh. That sounds nice." *Rather, it sounds like a chance to get out of this hellhole.* "Sure."

He nods and gestures for me to follow him down the winding staircase. He makes small-talk as we go, asking how I slept and how I'm feeling today, and mentions how nice the weather is today.

All the while, I keep focused on the layout of the tower, making note of anything that can help me escape when the time comes. I'll play nice with him for now, if it gets me more freedom and time to form a plan. I can feel the knife against my hip as we go down the stairs.

We eventually reach the entrance hallway and I see the two main doors are open. My heart jumps at the sight of the horse and carriage outside. There are also two horses with saddles on them. I quickly survey the area and see there are no guards around us. We are alone at this moment.

This is it. My chance. I just have to get on one of those horses and I'll be free to make my way out of the town. I've heard that the main entrance to the town faces the direction of the Kingdom, so in theory, I just need to leave and keep my bearings. I'll be safe once I'm out of the enemy's hands, at least.

"Ah..." I say, coming to a stop in the hall.

Lord Bearon stops and looks at me.

My pulse pounds in my temple. Can I really do this? Can I really use the knife on him? But I'll need to make sure he can't follow me or alert the guards once I'm on the move.

"What is it?" he asks.

I hate how concerned he sounds, and how pouty his lips are.

"I... I'm allergic to horses," I manage to get out, the lie slipping off my tongue weakly, just as bashful as I wished it to sound.

That gets him to turn around to regard the horses.

My hand is shaking as it slips into my dress and grips the knife.

Lord Bearon turns back to me and says, "You don't have to worry about—"

Without thinking, and hardly aware of my actions, I force my hand to whip out. The knife flashes and cuts through the air towards Lord Bearon's throat. One slash is all I need.

A brawny hand catches the knife an inch from his throat. For a long moment, we both stand there, frozen in time. Me with the knife and him holding my hand.

His face barely registers any shock.

I hardly know what I'm doing when I yank my hand away from him and prepare to go for another strike. But the side of my finger is nicked by the blade, and I gasp, dropping the knife with a clatter.

Lord Bearon acts fast and reaches out to take my hand. My first thought is that he's going to break the wrist or yank me away to haul me into the dungeon again. Instead, his hands are gentle when he examines my bleeding finger.

"It's a shallow cut," he says, holding my hand. "Are you okay?"

I stare at him, dumbfounded. "Am I okay?" I just tried to kill him, *twice*, and he's concerned about a tiny slice on my finger.

I'm aware of his hands encompassing mine, and how tender he is. I feel like I've been spun around and the world is teetering around me, and don't know what to think anymore.

He runs a gentle finger over my cut, and it has mostly stopped bleeding already.

"Yes, *Allspice*, are you okay? We can find some ointment in town if it begins to bother you. Just let me know."

"I... okay. I'm..." I have no capacity to form a sentence.

He even smiles at me, his beard shifting up. "Come on, let's show you the town." He pauses, half-turned, and adds, "Oh, and Clio—please do not try to kill me again. It would terribly dampen our day together."

My only response is a shaky nod to that.

He smiles again and leads the way out of the tower, into the bright daylight.

Chapter Thirteen

CLIO

It's a good thing I hadn't killed Lord Bearon and tried to escape, as there were stable hands just outside of the doors, tending to the horses. I wouldn't have gotten far at all before finding myself on the ground, dead alongside him.

Just as I step outside with him, two of his guards appear to leave with us. My mind is spinning at the idea of what could have just happened. There's no way I would have gotten far at all in my daring escape.

I sit out on the front driver's seat of the carriage beside Lord Bearon, who takes the reins, while his two guards sit inside the carriage. He explains he wants to take the carriage since he has a few things to collect from the markets in town. He doesn't address the fact that I'd just tried to kill him and escape, which somehow makes things even more awkward.

I find a long wool sweater on my passenger side seat, and Lord Bearon tells me it's in case I get a chill, which is an oddly kind gesture from him. It makes what I'd just attempted to do even worse.

We make our way down the winding rock paths leading away from the tower on the cliff top. When we turn a corner, we're greeted with a view of the entire town below. It's my first proper look at the Oathlands and I have to admit that it takes my breath away.

The town is much bigger in scope than the depictions I've seen, with sections rising and lowering on enormous hills. I would call this a city, so I wonder why they call it a town. It doesn't reach even half the heights of the Kingdom, and everything looks more modest and urban, with fewer extravagances, but it's still an impressive sight.

The buildings and streets look tightly packed together from above. Far to one side, I see the gleaming water of the River Zyne which borders the Oathlands. It's like all the sketches and paintings I've ever seen come to life, tenfold.

I tie my hair back after some time of the wind blowing it about. My long hair is wild and wavy and the curls are starting to come out. It's in dire need of a wash and brush, but somehow that doesn't bother me as much as I thought it would. As much as it used to.

Out of the corner of my eye, I notice Lord Bearon watching me fix my hair.

"Didn't your mother ever teach you not to stare?" I ask, half-joking.

He smiles and says, "You really do have quite an unusual hair color. It reminds me of someone I used to know."

"Oh, yeah? An old girlfriend?" I blush as soon as the words are out. "Sorry. You don't have to answer that."

He looks ahead and seems content in not answering. I can see him withdrawing into his thoughts. I'm conscious of the two guards in the carriage who can likely hear us.

You just apologized to your captor. You don't have to do that, I tell myself, but I don't fully believe the words, which disturbs me.

We finally reach the ground level and come out into a circular plaza that breaks off into three streets. We leave the horses and carriage to the side, beside a trough, and continue on foot.

"Are you not worried about anyone stealing the carriage or horses?" I ask, noting how he hasn't tied them up.

Lord Bearon chuckles lightly. "We Oathlanders look out for each other. We all have too much respect for one another to steal."

I look away to hide my surprise. That shows me how different things are in the Kingdom. Theft isn't a huge issue for us, but it is an almost daily occurrence. Pickpockets and such. But there are just too many people to police and watch out for all at once.

His two guards follow us at enough of a distance that I don't need to check on them.

Many people smile and wave at Lord Bearon as we walk, with many more that simply stare in awe. It's almost as though I'm back in the Kingdom with everyone staring at their princess, except all eyes are on him.

"Are you sure you're not royalty?" I ask.

Lord Bearon responds, "We haven't had royalty for over a hundred years."

I think back to the history books and recall their last Queen was Kristabelle Theokan. Her husband had gone mad and she'd withered in her old age. Apparently, there was no successor to the throne after that. I've often wondered if that was false history but I'm not too surprised to hear it's true. So the Oathlands really are led by their military these days.

We explore the streets, seeing small coffee shops, eateries, and many stalls and markets. The people here all seem polite and happy, and many offer us things to eat and drink. I have to admit that they're not at all what I imagined. Not that I'd imagined uncivilized savages, exactly, but still...

I have to laugh when two children run around our feet, giggling and yelling excitedly as they chase a puppy. I've always been in awe of small animals, and small people, and their laughter makes me miss my home.

Lord Bearon catches my withdrawal. "Is something wrong?"

I shake my head. "Nothing. Your town is lovely."

My fear is that I'm beginning to let my guard down, and that makes me more wary. I can't forget the situation I'm in.

"How is your hand?" he asks, reaching half-way across the distance between us.

"My finger," I say, raising my hand, pulling it out of his reach. "It's fine, really. It doesn't need any attention." Or any reminders of me trying to kill you and escape. The flesh around the thin line on my finger has flushed and swollen a little, but I pay it no mind. It's certainly not the slashing I'd been trying to give his throat, so I suppose there's little to complain about.

He eyes me for a moment, and I can see his concern. It reminds me of the moment we shared when he'd wiped my cheek. I have to look away, already feeling my cheeks redden. I hate it when he looks at me like that.

I could never befriend an Oathlander. It simply cannot be possible. My family would never speak to me again. I doubt I'd even be allowed back in the Kingdom if I told them I'd met a nice Oathlander.

We pass by a hut off the side of the street, and I see a small family crowded together inside. In a second hut, some of the people are spilling out into the street. Their clothes are ragged and they have the weathered, emaciated look of the homeless. My heart aches to see the poor, ailing people. It makes me notice how everyone around us is slightly unkempt, perhaps with dirt on their faces, patched clothing, worn-out sandals, and knotted hair. It's subtle, but the more I see of them, the more I notice how unpolished they are.

"We also have problems with the homeless and less-abled," I say to Lord Bearon.

He takes so long to answer that I wonder if he's heard me. "I admit that I went to your people to steal seeds and grains from your supplies. I'd just wanted to give us a few more years."

"What do you mean?" I ask, frowning.

"Our land is not what it once was. I won't get into the details, but we're running out of resources. That is hard to deny. Our crops are dwindling and our fields are not flourishing as they used to. We need fresh soil and grains. We need a lot that we don't have. And we're running out of what we do have."

My mouth has fallen open. "I had no idea the situation was this bad for you."

He almost laughs. "And if you did, would your people do anything about it? Or would they come to watch us slowly die?"

I swallow uncomfortably.

"I often send food and supplies to the poorer communities," he says. "But times have gotten tough lately, and I haven't been able to help as much as I'd like. Whatever my cooks make for me and my staff, I ensure that they make extra, or distribute leftovers across the town. The dire situations of some people have become overwhelming. I have to admit, I don't know what to do."

He looks at me and adds, "And so in a desperate attempt to help, I convinced fifty of our soldiers to ride with me to your people, hoping to sneak in to take seeds and grains, and possibly even some gold if we could. But all I'd accomplished was more death and destruction, and possibly a war, if they retaliate."

I consider what he said. "You had good intentions, but were terribly misguided and foolish. You were right to disguise yourselves as bandits, but my bet is that they will think of your people as the culprits. It's the way of... *us*, unfortunately."

I've noticed that he hasn't said 'the Kingdom' out loud, and I catch myself before saying it. I guess he doesn't want to draw even more attention to us by saying those words.

Watching him now, I can't help but see him in a new light. A troubled soul who is only trying to do what he can to help his people. I can relate.

"You could have simply asked us for aid," I say.

He gives me a sour look. "Do you really think that would have worked?"

"No," I admit. "But what about asking someone else for help? Like Syraxia, Koprus, or the Sundown Isles?"

"The Kingdom has spread enough lies and propaganda against us that all the nearby lands have become sworn to them and enemies to us. None would consider coming to our aid."

I frown deeply. "I hadn't realized how ostracized the Oathlands had become. I thought your quarrels were mostly with the Kingdom. Not with the continent."

"Whatever the Kingdom says, the others follow," he says with bitterness coloring his voice.

We stop when a man in a soldier's uniform comes up to us. I recognize the Oathlands military colors of brown, gold, and black. There is a nervous edge to the man, as though he doesn't want to be seen speaking to Lord Bearon.

"Would you excuse us for a moment?" Lord Bearon says to me, and doesn't wait for an answer before he steps away with the man. They speak low enough for me not to hear their words.

That's the most secretive Lord Bearon has been with me so far. Not that I'd expect him to share everything with me. Even so, it troubles me to see the concerned, pained expression on him as he speaks to that soldier.

I look around and see a nearby market stall. Trinkets of many kinds are on display, hanging up or on a counter, along with jewelry and an assortment of odd charms.

A young man around my age lights up when he sees me, his eyes widening. He's in a baggy sweater with some loose stitching wide enough to make holes.

"Welcome, welcome. You are most welcome, my Lady," he says in a light, nervous voice on the brink of stuttering.

I see the way he's looking at me, which is the same as others often look, with their stares lingering for a bit too long. The gleam in their eyes. The way they look me up and down. This one seems harmless, at least.

He runs a hand over his curly brown hair, his round face cracking into a big smile. He has the scrawny look of someone who hardly eats well. But I like the fun, humorous air about him.

"Something pretty to match my Lady's beauty?" he asks, waving a hand over his wares. "Well, I'm afraid there is nothing to match that."

I smile demurely. "You're most kind. I'm just looking for now, thank you."

"I haven't seen you around here before. I'd know if I had."

I'm not quite sure what to tell him. "I'm just passing through." I hope that's close to the truth, anyway.

"Then you mustn't leave without a token to remember us by." He flicks up a finger to tell me to wait and turns to bend low behind the counter, rummaging through some boxes.

There is an old man sitting beside the stall. His white hair is flaring out wildly, and his overly large brown eyes are alive with keen intelligence. I feel compelled to step closer and say hello, noting that Lord Bearon is still huddled in a secret discussion with the soldier.

"I know you," he says, his voice soft and croaky. "Welcome back."

"This is my first time in the Oathlands," I say with a polite smile.

He frowns deeply, his entire face wrinkling. "That is not correct, young lady. For I know you very well. You are a very special person. Do you know that?"

My smile becomes bemused and I figure I can humor the old man. He must be mistaking me for someone in the past. "Ah, yes, thank you."

The young man interjects. "Eh, Grandpa, I was serving this customer."

"Self-serving, more like," the old man mutters under his breath.

"What's that?" the young man says, flustered. "Anyway, here you go, my Lady." He holds out a pendant with a dull emerald in the center, adorned with intricate silver engravings. "This once belonged to a beloved mayor in the Oathlands. Back when we had mayors. She'd sworn her family discovered it deep in the Moyesen Caves, out by land's end. This is a rare Ancient Koprus diamond."

"It's an emerald, you imbecile," the old man says.

"Shush, grandpa!" The young man's face flushes red, reminding me of an embarrassed child.

"That's not even Ancient Koprus. Go find her that ruby bracelet we keep in the back. You know the one with the gold and the chain we fixed up."

"That's a great idea," the young man says. He pauses and adds, "Hey, um... I'm Tokus, by the way."

"It's nice to meet you, Tokus," I say, and can see there isn't a polite way not to give my name back. "I'm Clio."

His eyes light up. "Clio. What a wonderful name. Do you know what it means?"

"I've been told it means *a gift from the gods*."

He nods enthusiastically and holds up that finger again, before rummaging through the trays in the boxes.

The old man reaches a gnarled hand out to me. I take his hand and see there is something in it. He drops a translucent crystal in my hand, about the size of a small apple, with pointed ends.

He leans closer and whispers hoarsely, "Come back to me when you can see the light inside. Only inspect it when you are alone."

His words sound ominous, but I slip the crystal into my pocket as his grandson, Tokus, comes back to us.

Lord Bearon also arrives and sees Tokus holding a silver bracelet with gold adornments, and a vibrant blood-red ruby encased in the center. There is a gap in one section which has a chain to open and fasten it.

"That looks lovely," Lord Bearon says. "We'll take it."

Tokus looks confused, and I can tell he's a little annoyed to have my focus taken from him. "I was... just about to let the lady try it on, my Lord."

"No need. I'm sure it fits well. How much would you like for it?"

Tokus humbly bows to Lord Bearon. "I wouldn't think to charge you, oh great Fireheart."

Lord Bearon brings out a handful of silver chips from his purse and places them on the counter. "A man should be paid for his wares."

Tokus nods appreciatively, looking away.

We go on our way, thanking Tokus, and the old man gives me a knowing look that sends a chill through me. I keep the crystal hidden in a pocket inside my dress.

Chapter Fourteen
CLIO

After we finish collecting a few blankets, tubs of paint, some fresh fruit, vegetables, and meats, Lord Bearon sends his guards back to load the wagon. He takes me up a hill beyond the markets to a villa that he promises serves some of the best food in town. Even after picking at a few things handed to me during our shopping, my stomach is grumbling for more sustenance, and a lot of water.

The owner of the restaurant greets us both like old friends.

"It's been far too long, my Lord," he says, frowning at Lord Bearon. To me, he adds, "People say he's a recluse, hiding away in his tower. But I say he just likes his privacy, aye? And who could blame him, when he's everyone's favorite topic of gossip." The man laughs at his own joke, patting his round stomach and grinning before turning, giving us a simple gesture to follow.

We're led to a white-clothed table with a view of rolling fields. Beyond the greenery is another part of the town, with tall silver buildings that could be factories. The sun is creeping over the villa, pushing away the shadows, and will eventually reach us, but there is no chill in the shade.

There is a quaint rural feel to the place, with the branches of low-hanging trees nestled overhead to create a roof. Small fruit hangs from the branches, not ripened enough to pick. There is a fresh smell in the air, like cut grass or dewy leaves.

"I will return with our finest bottle of wine to get you started," the owner says.

I notice the white cloth is a little worn and the wooden chairs have likely seen better days. Like most things I've seen, they're nice, but I can see how old and frail they've become. It points out what Lord Bearon has said about their resources running out, and how their people have been struggling lately.

"A recluse, huh?" I say once we're left alone at the table.

"People like to talk about me a lot," Lord Bearon says. "They have a lot of names for me."

"Like Fireheart? Your soldiers called you that, too, I remember."

He makes a sour face. "Some names are better than others. Many here think highly of me. Whether or not that's justified is up to them."

"You help your people a lot," I say. "I can appreciate that. And relate. But why do you hide in your tower so much?" *And relate*. Shit. It probably would have been best to leave that part out.

Lord Bearon doesn't seem to think much of it, though. He surveys the scenery. "How about we enjoy the view?"

"That's called deflecting," I say. "And it's a terrible attempt at it."

He half frowns and smiles. "I'm afraid I'll just bore you with details of my life."

"What about that soldier who stopped you just now? He seemed to have a lot to say to you."

Lord Bearon frowns again, his sharp brows crinkling. "He was one of the men who went with me. One of the ones who came back. He's been having issues with his family, and the oaths he swore to the Oathlands. He regretted his actions and needed me to reassure him we did what we thought was best. He wasn't in a good place after what we'd done. After losing those that didn't come back."

I can see the turmoil raging in his eyes. The depth of dealing with what he did. And those affected along with him. It surprises me how casual Lord Bearon appears at times, and it's only sometimes that I can see a glimpse of the trauma inside him.

"You mentioned a Lady Moira to me before," I say, wanting to learn more about him. "I saw a portrait of Moira Alecante. Is that who you meant?"

He appears shaken for a moment, as though stunned. There's a lot going on behind his dark eyes. So much conflict and turmoil. "This is not the right moment for that subject."

"Why not? Who is she? You brought her up."

"I shouldn't have," he says softly.

"Is she your wife? *Was* your wife? As you might have guessed, I won't give up easily."

"Yes, I see that very clearly," he says, and leans forward with his elbows on the table. He looks about us for a moment, I guess to find his words. When he speaks, his voice is low.

"Moira Alecante was my mother. She would have been Queen of the Oathlands if her mother and father, Elona and Harris Theokan, had not disbanded the throne."

"I thought Kristabelle Theokan was the last royal ruler of the Oathlands."

"That's what we wanted everyone to think. Because for a time they believed that our royal line was cursed, and none wanted the throne. Harris and Elona ruled for a time, but in secret, until they decided there should no longer be royalty in the Oathlands. They wanted to live their lives safely, without the fear of constant threats. When my mother married, she took her husband's last name, Alecante, wanting to distance herself even more from the throne."

I frown as I listen to him. "Why did they think the throne was cursed?"

"Because whoever sat on the throne only knew death and chaos in their lives."

"I'm sure our royal family has suffered as much as yours over the centuries of fighting."

He shakes his head, his face twisting into a scowl. "That is not true. Please, can we talk about something else?"

"Is there something I should know?" I ask, sensing how angry he's getting. "Please, tell me."

He looks out at the fields as he speaks. "I asked you about Lady Moira to see if you'd heard of her. The Last Blood War didn't begin because the Oathlands attacked first, trying to gain control of the Kingdom. That's what everyone was told. The truth is that your king sent spies to assassinate my mother."

"That's a lie," I snap. "King Zias would never do such a thing."

Lord Bearon shrugs, as if it is a truth and nothing else. "There isn't much he won't do. Him, or those that came before him. I'm telling you the truth that's been kept from you and your people. My mother began to make plans to gain her rightful throne back. The Kingdom throne. And when your king found out about this, he had her killed. That's how the Last Blood War began."

"Why would your mother think she had a claim to the throne? I don't understand."

"The history is long and difficult to explain, and I fear you won't believe what I say, anyway. But the rightful claim was hers. And, just like how the First Blood War began by Kingdom deeds, and later blamed on the Oathlands, so the Last Blood War started."

"You're right," I say defiantly. "I won't believe what you say. I'm sure *you* believe it, however. And I can't fault that. I guess we both have sides that we see. Who's to say which is right or wrong?"

"Indeed. Your taught history says one thing...and the truth says another."

A fire burns within me, particularly at the high-and-mighty air about him. "You think you know it all, you Oathlanders. Have you ever stopped to think that maybe you have history skewed? Perhaps us Kingdom folk are not to blame for as much as you put on us?"

He has a sad, forlorn smile on him that almost makes me feel bad for snapping at him. "Your temper matches your hair," is all he says.

I'm not sure what to say about that, but I'm too riled up to let things go. "You think you're all better than us, don't you? You Oathlanders who look out for each other? What about those who are sworn to protect you all? Your military? Did you know your soldiers threatened to have their way with me?"

His eyes narrow.

"That's right. While I was a captive in the wilderness. Oh, how they laughed at what they could do to me. I didn't sleep that night. I was too afraid for one of them to grow bold enough to grab me in the darkness."

"You must have misinterpreted their words, or mistook their jests—"

"Of course you'd take their side."

"I'm not. I'm just saying maybe you—"

"Yes, maybe the fault is with me. Just like our kingdom's faults are with us, and not on you."

"I never said we were innocent in this," he says sternly.

I match his anger. "Then stop trying to convince me that we're the villains in your story."

He pauses and visibly calms down, his voice lowering. "We are both the heroes and the villains. That is the way of things."

I shake my head, frustrated with talking to him.

The restaurant owner is by the doorway, clearly not wanting to disturb us.

But someone does come to disturb us. A uniformed soldier. A different one than the man who'd spoken with Lord Bearon earlier.

"My Lord," the soldier says hurriedly, his agitation heaving his shoulders. He looks like he's run to us. "Kingdom scouts have been seen on our borders. General Commander Rourk requests your presence."

My wide-eyed look meets Lord Bearon dark eyes. If this is true, that means my people are on their way to me. But then, that would mean war is coming with them.

"I'll be at the garrison immediately," Lord Bearon says to the soldier, and dismisses him.

"Do you think there really are Kingdom scouts out there?" I ask.

"If there are, it doesn't necessarily mean an army is with them. Scouts are a regular occurrence. Maybe the Kingdom is merely looking around. Possibly looking for you. It doesn't have to mean war. But it..."

"It doesn't look good," I finish for him. For a second, I'm racked with stress and fear before I remember I am not one of them. I am a prisoner here, and an attack on their town would mean my eventual freedom.

So why do I feel so bad for them?

"Please," Lord Bearon says. "Stay here. Have whatever you like on the menu. As much as you can eat and drink. I'll send for my guards to escort you back to the tower whenever you're ready. I recommend some grape juice, seeing how ripe they are."

He nods to a bunch of grapes hanging from a vine, and I turn around to see them. I'm mostly turned in my seat when I hear a sharp intake of breath.

I spin around to him. "What is it?"

The color has drained from Lord Bearon's face. He stares at me as if he's only noticing me for the first time.

"What?" I say again. "What is it?"

"You have a mark on the back of your shoulder," he says, breathing heavily.

"Oh. Yes, I do," I say. "It's a birthmark. Why?"

A chill runs through me from the way he's looking at me.

He swallows. "I've just... never seen it before. May I have a look?"

"Why?" I'm immediately on the defensive.

"For curiosity's sake. One might say you owe me, after your little stunt earlier." He raises an expectant eyebrow.

I'm hesitant, but I turn my shoulder to him. He spends a moment inspecting my small birthmark, which has always been unremarkable to me.

"It looks a little like a star, right?" I say. "Sometimes it's clearer in the daylight."

He doesn't say anything. When I turn to him, he is frowning deeply, and his face has gone ashen white. I want to ask what he's thinking, but Lord Bearon strides away without another word.

Chapter Fifteen

CLIO

I withdraw to my rooms that evening, finding myself contemplating the bizarre, troubling events of the past few days. I still can't fully comprehend that I'm a prisoner of the Oathlands. It all feels like a strange dream and I keep expecting to wake up to find myself in bed with Leonas, curled into his side. Safe.

After bathing and dressing in a nightgown, I sit at the nightstand and brush my hair, looking into the round mirror. I sorely miss the amenities and toiletries I'm used to having in my room, but I'm making do with what I have here. At least I'm not back in a cell.

Lord Bearon's dark, brooding eyes come to mind. I've been thinking about him a lot lately. I understand now that he had come to the Kingdom under dire circumstances and he had meant no harm to us. An Oathlander coming to the Kingdom without harm in their hearts is a strange new concept for me. For anyone.

I hate to think of these people running out of resources and potentially reaching starvation. That should never happen to anyone. I know the Kingdom has favor across the lands, but I haven't ever considered that means the Oathlands would be out of favor with them.

It isn't like the Oathlanders are completely innocent, though. They've brought death and destruction to the Kingdom for centuries. They were the ones who started the bitter rivalry by attacking first all that time ago. Everyone knows that. My great grandparents had both been killed during one of the many battles between our lands, and I know of many people whose friends and family members have died at an Oathlander's hands.

So why can't I stop feeling bad for them?

I regard the bundles of clothes I'd set aside on a chair, and go to them. Within the folds of the dress I'd worn today is the crystal that the old man had given me. I haven't given it much thought as I figured it's just a trinket and maybe not even real crystal, but I examine it now and see that it's quite remarkable, and sturdy. The crystal has a lot of depth to it and I can feel myself getting lost within its facets. It is perhaps the loveliest piece of jewelry I've seen. The most remarkable, certainly.

The old man had told me to go back to him when I see the light in the crystal, or something like that. I'm not quite sure what he meant, but I hold it up to the light overhead. There doesn't seem to be anything interesting to see, and the light doesn't reach far into the crystal. It mostly bounces off it.

I catch myself and shake my head. What am I doing? I shouldn't be entertaining the fancies of a strange old Oathlander. I shouldn't even be *here*.

The Founding Festival is coming up soon. I was meant to have it all planned by now. I wonder if it's even going ahead without me there. Well, of course it would. We celebrated the Founding Festival every year. It will not get canceled just because the niece of the king is missing.

I can still hear the cries of that young girl in the back of the wagon. Should I have just left her there? It would mean I'd be home right now. But then, that girl would have been brought here in my place.

Perhaps I was meant to have been brought to the Oathlands, to see how they live. To get a glimpse of the enemy's true face.

A vibrating sensation washes over me. The crystal in my hands begins to thrum. I look down to see a dim glow. There is a white light emanating from within the crystal. The sight of it startles me and I sit up, almost dropping the crystal. Then the light disappears as though it had never been there.

Did I really just see what I think I saw? Maybe it was a trick of the light. Is this what the old man had wanted me to see? I examine the crystal again, trying to decipher where that light had come from.

What had that thrumming sensation been? Had that come from the crystal or from me? I shiver at the prospect of either.

I decide that's enough for one day, and nestle the crystal back within the bundle of clothes.

As I turn from the chair, I glimpse out the window across the room and freeze. Out in the darkness, the shape of that enormous creature can be seen. It is far in the distance beyond the trees, and would be hard to detect against the darkness were it not for its red eyes. It is simply standing there, hunched on its hind legs, up on a cliff top. My heart is racing, but I'm relieved that the window is closed, at least. Although I doubt that a pane of glass would do much to stop that thing from coming in if it wanted.

I change my mind about the crystal's resting spot and place it in a drawer beside my bed instead. When I look back at the window, the red eyes of the beast are no longer there but I think I see something swiftly moving through the darkness. But that might just be my eyes playing tricks on me.

I make a mental note to tell Lord Bearon about that lurking creature as I close the curtains and climb into bed. I'm hoping to get a good night's sleep, despite my danger senses pulsing.

Chapter Sixteen

Arthur

I've been with the old wise woman for almost two hours now, and I've yet to find what I'm looking for. The heavy odor of dust is in the air, the specks of which are twinkling in the firelight from the lanterns around us. The smothering smell of sweat and incense from the old woman, trapped in the confines of the large study, is also hard to ignore.

"Are you sure you are in the correct place for what you seek?" she asks, her glistening orbs of eyes watching me closely. Her gnarled face is bordered by her long, frizzled gray hair as she leans on the desk.

"Can we ever truly know that?" I ask, knowing she likes to speak in philosophical terms.

That earns me a big grin.

I've explained that I'm looking for specific information that I don't think I'll find in my personal library. This old woman, Elazra, is known for having treasures of the past that no one else does. Possibly because she is the oldest person in the Oathlands. So old that no one actually knows how old she is. Whenever someone asks her age, she gives a different answer each time. My guess is a little over a hundred.

I'm looking through a book on magical artifacts and creatures, which is written as a real historical journal rather than a work of fiction. I glance over a page about sirens, who were known to entice men to their doom. I don't know if what I'm looking for is in here, but I've exhausted the more obvious books.

Elazra jabs a bony finger onto the page. "A siren attempted to entice me once. I had to stick my head inside a beehive to protect myself from its manipulative words."

I frown at that. "Oh, really? That must have been a painful experience."

She shrugs, raising both hands. "The stinging of the bees told me I still had control over myself. Better than succumbing to the siren."

I shake my head, having heard enough of the old woman's crazy stories over the years, and return to the book.

The next page details the Fae, who were an ancient race of fairy-like people, known to have powerful magical abilities.

"Did you ever meet one of these Fae?" I ask absently.

"No, but I did meet a dark wizard who was on the run from the Fae, who wanted to punish him for some dark deed. He trapped me in a bottle. But, that was just a misunderstanding, and we became good friends after that. Oh, but that was so long ago."

"How long ago?" I ask.

She ponders that with a deep frown. "Somewhere over a hundred and fifty years, I'd wager."

I stare at her. "Elazra. Just how old are you?"

Her response is a knowing grin.

After a time of looking through the book, she asks, "Would you tell me what you're really looking for?"

I'm running out of options and I'd rather not spend the entire night here with the old woman, so I take a chance and tell her the truth.

"What do you know about the symbol of a star with a hole in the center?"

"Ahhh. The mark of the royal family."

That's right. Every member of the Oathland's royal family in line to the throne were marked with the symbol from birth.

"And only those in line to the throne would have this birthmark?" I ask skeptically. "So if a niece or cousin of the Queen was born, they wouldn't have this mark?"

"That is correct. The birthmarks were steeped in old magic. But that magic died out long before the royal family dissolved."

That's probably why Rourk and I don't have the birthmarks. Not that we were expected to take the throne at any point. I don't think my mother or father had one either. If there was ever any contention in the past as to who should rule the Oathlands, the person with the birthmark would be seen as the rightful seat on the throne. At least, that's how people used to see things.

"Does anyone have this birthmark nowadays?" I ask.

She cocks her head curiously. "Well... no one would have *this* mark. The line to the throne has ended. If you found this mark on someone, well, then they would have claim to our throne. And the Kingdom would not be happy about us reforging our royal lineage."

I frown in thought, taking in her words.

"I tell you what," she says with what could pass as a smile. "I will perform an old ritual for you." She begins rummaging through sacks and boxes cluttered nearby. "This will tell us if there is magic in the air. I like to perform it every now and then, just for fun."

"Has this ever shown the existence of magic?"

Elazra shrugs and shakes her head, her frizzy hair wavering. "Never. But I am an old fool who has not forgotten how to hope."

She places a bowl on the table before us and crumbles a coarse powder into it.

"There was a time when the Oathlands was a place of magic and wonder. Our people have lost this magic over the years, to the extent that you kids these days don't know of your magical heritage."

"I'm almost forty," I tell her. "Hardly a ki—"

"During my youth," she continues, ignoring me, "ogres and centaurs and wizards walked the streets, and witches and fairies roamed the skies. Then, the Kingdom began killing as many of our magical beings as they could, to even out the battlefield. Those Kingdom folk were never born with magic in their blood, and that annoyed their old kings greatly."

"I've heard the bedtimes stories," I say, watching her drop flakes of something into the bowl, then pour what I believe to be oil in there. "No one actually believes them to be true. Except for you."

"No one is as smart as me." She finishes by taking a pinch of a dark powder from a pouch and holds her fist over the bowl. "Are you ready?"

"Do I need to do anything?"

"No."

"Then I'm ready."

She grins and drops the powder into the bowl. Nothing happens. My shoulders sag. I don't know what I'd been expecting, but–

A puff of blue light ignites from the bowl, so vivid and clear, but just for a second. Then it disappears, leaving an afterimage in my eyes. The air is still, as though nothing had disturbed it, save for a faint wisp of smoke lingering over the bowl.

I'm stunned, and I look up to see Elazra with an elated grin on her face, her eyes wider and more alive than I've ever seen.

"Well," she says. "How about that?"

Chapter Seventeen

CLIO

I wake up with a start, my heart racing. All around me is the dull darkness of the bedroom.

I had dreamt that my father had come to the Oathlands, but he hadn't wanted to rescue me. He'd seen me as one of them and had chosen to leave me here. I had been running for him, screaming to take me back, when I'd tripped and fell into the mud. That's when I'd awoken.

I hear the pattering of rain hitting the window. I look over to see the curtain is slowly billowing. I don't recall opening the window...

I instantly feel as though I'm not alone in the room. My most primal instincts are set aflame, warning me of danger from deep in my stomach, my very bones.

I cautiously look over the dark room, seeing sections highlighted by the faint moonlight coming in, and see a shadow come alive in the darkness. The beast with the red eyes is in the room.

I scream as it lunges for me. Scrambling away, I leap out as it crashes into the bed, crumpling the frame. I'm aware of it becoming tangled in the sheets, growling as it attempts to free itself, while I throw myself to my feet and rush towards the doorway.

My breath is sharp and strained as I run through the lounge room and head for the main doors. The beast crashes into the room and begins charging towards me, smashing a table and knocking over chairs. The massive thing leaps and swings a claw at me, but I duck and dive to the side. It crashes into a cabinet, throwing out glass and wood, and hits the wall while I duck for safety behind a sofa.

I peek out and see it clearly now as it gathers itself, huffing and snarling. It is a heaving, bear-like creature with the snout and ears of a wolf. Its bulging arms are twice as long as its legs, and its hands could easily wrap around my body. The milky moonlight streaming in highlights grey-blue fur and gleaming sharp ivory teeth. It stands tall at over eight feet, as wide as three men. A thunderous roar bursts from its enormous mouth and my blood chills.

Its glowing eyes catch me ducking back behind the sofa. In an instant, it lunges for me and crashes into the sofa, knocking it over just as I scramble away. It must have its claws stuck in the sofa as it takes a second to be free from it, and I take that extra second to reach the front doors. I throw them open and burst out into the hallway, almost hitting the wall ahead.

There are no guards around. No one down the long hallway that spreads out behind and ahead. I pump my legs and race towards the staircase at the end of the hall, not daring to look back.

Where is everyone? Surely they must be alert to the raging beast devastating my rooms. I yell for help and pray someone hears me.

The creature crashes through the doors and begins chasing me, huffing and growling. I turn to see it running on all fours like a wild, rabid animal. It's incredibly fast and is upon me in seconds.

I turn and scream, falling back as the beast flies through the air towards me, its claws reaching out. When I throw my hands up protectively, a blinding light flashes. For a moment, I'm lost in the fiery light, and it takes some time to blink back my focus to see I'm alone in the hallway. I don't know what's just happened, but I can hear the heavy footfalls of the creature running through the halls. Or that could be the throbbing of my temple and my furiously beating heart.

What just happened? Where had that light come from?

After what could be a minute or a half hour, I come out of my daze to hear someone is coming for me. I feel a hand grab my shoulder from behind. I scream shrilly and burst into panic-mode, but then see that it's Lord Bearon. He has come for me. I allow myself to melt into his powerful arms as he kneels beside me.

He is calming and I am a wreck, shaken from my ordeal. I gratefully nestle into his warm embrace. He holds me close, and for a moment, all the fear and anxiety melts away.

Chapter Eighteen

CLIO

After a rough, strange night of sleeping in a small guest room, with several guards posted in and outside of the room, I have the strong urge to go out for a walk in the sunshine, despite feeling drained. The morning has brought with it a fresh start, and it has sparked something in me. A need to get some answers.

It had taken all of my energy to convince Lord Bearon not to sleep on the floor beside my bed. He'd wanted to stay close in case that creature came back for me. I reluctantly like the attention and comfort, but I would not have been able to sleep knowing he was in the same room.

After going back up to my devastated rooms to retrieve the crystal from the drawer, I've made my way to the front gardens of the tower. I'm aware of at least four guards following me, some of them more obvious than others.

I intend to explore as much of the town as I can, to get a lay of the land. My aim is to see which routes lead out of town, and get a rough idea of how I can go from Lord Bearon's tower to the town outskirts, ideally on horseback.

When I reach the front gate at the edge of the gardens, the guards pick up their pace and call for me to stop.

"Apologies, Lady Welling," the nearest guard says. He is older than many of the others, in his fifties, with a steel look in his eyes and a solid bearing. "We have strict instructions not to let you leave the tower grounds."

I hold my chin high. "After last night's attack, Lord Bearon has permitted me leave to explore the town. You may all accompany me, of course."

They exchange looks.

"We... were not told of this, ma'am," the older man says.

"What is your name?" I ask him.

"Cheston, ma'am," he says with a stiff nod. "Cheston Haversham."

"Well, Cheston Haversham. I explained to Lord Bearon that I no longer feel safe couped up in that tower all day, and we agreed I'd be able to wander the town, with supervision. You may go check with him, but I will continue on with my day. So, you can either follow me or go and check with him, and waste everyone's time, in which case you'd then have to try and find me in town. Now, would you rather lose sight of the person you've been tasked with following, or check what I'm telling you while I'm out there, all alone?"

The four men seem unsure, and a little bewildered, but eventually they agree to keep following me into town. I continue on, relieved that my ruse worked.

The winding path into town takes me over an hour to get through. I don't think I've ever walked so much in a day in my entire life, as I'm used to taking a wagon everywhere. The Kingdom is large enough that no one ever walks far without taking transport. I should have chosen better footwear for this kind of walking, especially with the rocky, uneven ground.

At times, the guards follow too closely, hovering like shadows, and one time one of them even stumbles and bumps into me. I have to stop and ask them to keep more of a distance and not crowd me. Thankfully, they do as I ask. Their responsiveness makes me feel like I'm still the princess in the Kingdom, even if no one knows that here.

When I reach the familiar market street I'd visited yesterday, I find the trinket stall, looking for that strange old man who had given me the crystal. Instead, I see that young man again with the curly brown hair and spotted face. His eyes light up when he sees me.

"Oh, it's you, my lady," he says excitedly, coming out from behind the stall. "How are you on this beautiful morning? Ah, may I get you a sweater, to fight the morning chill?"

I smile appreciatively. "Thank you, but I'm fine. I've always had a way of regulating my body. Never too cold in winter, never too hot in summer."

"You are very special, indeed. In many ways." His eyes dart toward my less than considerable cleavage and settle on my lips. "Ah, please, can I offer you a drink? I was just about to go get myself one."

He's trying hard to be nice, which is sweet, but I've found it best not to encourage men like him too much, to avoid them getting the wrong idea.

"You're very kind, but I'm okay, thank you. I was actually looking for that older man that was with you, yesterday."

He doesn't hide his disappointed frown. "My granddad? He's not here. He wakes up late most days. He's with my little brother at home. I suspect he'll be showing up in a few hours, though. You're welcome to wait here for him."

I really would rather not spend that much time with this young man, whose eyes keep straying and who I can't be sure if I trust. "Oh, that's okay, thank you. I'll try to come round later then." I decide to take a chance on him and bring out the crystal. "Can you tell me what you know about this?"

He straightens, his jaw dropping. "Oh, wow. Where'd you get this? This is... wow. This is very old. And rare."

"I found it in my grandmother's attic," I lie.

"This is a Fae crystal," he says. "We have one, too. But I've never seen another one before."

"A Fae crystal?" I ask. "What is that?"

He gives me a quizzical look as though he's trying to decipher why I'm really here, but then seems to relax. "Well, you see, these things could once channel magic, and could heighten the magic of those around them. But, that was in the old days, and to be honest, I think they're just stories that everyone's grandparents used to tell them. They fetch a *high* price, though."

"Someone told me that it could emit a light," I say casually. "What does that mean?"

"You know your artifacts," he says, impressed. "The white light is when a magic user channels their magic through it. But, of course, no one alive has ever seen that. Your friend who told you has probably read the same magic books as me. You know..." he leans in conspiratorially, "some people think that magic is just in the old stories, but I think it was once very real. My granddad used to have a powerful magic in him, but that magic died out along with everyone else's over the years."

"Why did the magic die?" I ask, doing my best to keep from sounding too curious, so he doesn't get any ideas about using my need for his knowledge to his advantage. I'm not sure what kind of man he is, but I do know that I would really rather not test his limits—or mine.

"Because the sources of magic died. That was the Fae. Without any of them left in the world, magic eventually faded away. Everyone thinks they're myths because they died out so long ago. The Fae were like power sources for magic. When they were around, people all over were able to learn and wield magic. And there used to be magical creatures in the world, like dragons and flying horses. But the Kingdom killed all the Fae and over the years, the magic just... went away."

I take in his words with a thoughtful look, and notice his expression lightening.

"But you don't have to worry about all of that," he says cheerily. "You look hungry. How about we go for some breakfast? My treat."

"That's kind of you, but I must be going. I'll try to return later to speak with your grandfather."

"I'll be here, too," he says with a needy smile.

I consider giving him back the crystal, but I don't want his grandfather to get in trouble for giving it out to me. So I hold on to it for now.

I wish him a good day and continue down the street. A cup of coffee does sound good, I decide. I look around for Lord Bearon's guards and only see one of them in eye view. I could ask them for directions to the nearest coffee stall, but instead I keep wandering, not minding the feeling of being lost. That's part of the fun of exploring.

There is a lot to mull over about what that young man had said. Does he really believe in all that stuff about Fae and dragons and magic? I'm guessing his grandfather's stories have gotten to him.

My head clears the more I walk, and I feel free despite my followers. It's an odd feeling, to be free while captive in enemy territory. Except that it doesn't feel like I'm in enemy territory. Although that's likely because they don't know who I am. They see me as whoever they want me to be.

When I look back, it takes me a while to spot any of the guards following me. I guess they really are trying not to bother me, and keeping their distance. Not that there's much to fear in this town. The crowds are growing and the streets are getting busier, but I see no unsavory-types or feel any sense of danger.

When I walk by a side street, I notice a frail, scared-looking black and white cat. I can't help but follow it, wanting to see if it needs anything. But after a few steps into the side street, I lose sight of the cat when it darts around a corner. I hurry to keep up and turn the corner in time to see the cat hop onto a barrel and jump over a chain fence. That leaves me with a dead-end. My shoulders sag, but I'm relieved to see the cat seems to be okay. Just a little scared of me, most likely. But I can't help it, I've always had a thing for strays and those less fortunate.

I head back out of the alley towards the street, but stop when I see three large men turning the corner, coming to me. The one in the middle is the tallest, with an open vest that stretches over his hairy barrel chest. The other two are big and muscled, looking just as menacing as the first.

"Look at this, lads," the tallest one says with a slimy grin. The features of his broad face are somewhat pinched together. Eyes too close, mouth too high. "We caught ourselves a right prize piece."

The other two chuckle at that. My heart jumps when I see the knife in one of their hands. I quickly look around but see there is no way out but through the men.

Stupid, stupid, I think, cursing myself. Why did I have to go and follow that damn cat?

My only hope is that Lord Bearon's guards saw me go into the side street, but with the crowds outside, there's a chance they've lost me. Now, around the corner of the street in a dead-end alley, there's a chance no one will hear me if I yell. And yelling may only anger these men into action.

"Please, I don't want any trouble," I tell them, my lips quivering. "I'm just passing through. My father, he is very sick, and he needs urgent—"

"He's gonna have to wait, isn't he?" the one with the knife says. His eyes flash with something chaotic, and I get the impression he is a little unhinged.

"I don't have much coin," I say, "but you can have whatever I—"

"We don't want your coin, little lady," the tallest man says, making a show of licking his lips. "Come here."

He reaches a meaty hand out. I try to evade him, but he's too big and too fast, and he grabs hold of my blouse. The third man, without the knife, wraps his arms around me and lifts me off my feet. The tallest slaps a sweaty hand over my mouth. I desperately kick out, but there is little I can do with my arms pinned at my sides, and I'm no match for their strength. I make a weak attempt at kicking my captor's shins, but that only makes them laugh. My screams are muted against the hand over my mouth.

"Let's shut her up," the tallest says.

The man with the knife steps closer, bringing the blade up with glee in his mad eyes.

I kick out with all my might, but it's useless. There's nothing I can do against them.

Something large falls from above and crashes into the man with the knife. I'm thrown back with the impact and hit my head on the ground. I can hear the sounds of struggling and shuffling feet, and a heavy body drops. Through my dazed, pained vision, I see the newcomer attacking the men.

It's Lord Bearon. I don't know how he found me, and I'm not so sure that I care. I'm just immensely grateful, the weight of his protection and the safety it provides me instantly lifting a weight off my shoulders.

He grabs the man who had a hold of me and throws him into the wall, bones crunching with the impact. Lord Bearon is surprisingly vicious as he attacks the men and moves with such speed and strength that I hardly recognize him. He spins around and unloads a barrage of punches into the tallest man, before lifting him up by the throat and slamming him to the ground. He darts towards the knife wielder and swings a powerful uppercut that sends the man several feet into the air, the knife clattering to the ground when he lands.

Lord Bearon stands over three fallen bodies, all of whom are groaning or wincing in pain. He has his broad back to me, his shoulders heaving, and for a moment I feel like I don't recognize him. Especially when he turns and I first meet his eyes. I see a great, horrible darkness in his eyes that makes me gasp.

But his entire being softens when he steps to me, and I see the kind, protective man again.

"Are you okay? Are you hurt?" he says as he kneels beside me.

This is the second time in two days that he's come to my aid, and the second time that I gratefully melt into his arms. I hold him close, shivering and breathing him in, relieved to have him there.

We stay in each other's arms for a long time.

Chapter Nineteen
CLIO

The sun has begun to set by the time Lord Bearon and I make our way up the roof of his tower.

It amazes me that there is a flat section at the very top of the tower with stair access, but that's not nearly as amazing as the view. All around, the sky is on fire with reds and oranges highlighting the clouds, pierced by shafts of sun rays.

It's easily the highest I've ever been and I can see the vast, rolling landscape in all directions. Lord Bearon gestures towards where the Kingdom is, hidden behind a vast mountain range that looks no taller than my thumbnail. The dark tower is not the tallest of buildings in town, but its position high on the cliff makes it the highest point. Despite the height and the lack of railing or walls around us, I'm not afraid because I'm with him.

I have spent the past few hours with him making sure I'm alright after my ordeal. There was a large scrape on my forearm which I don't remember getting, so he had cleaned the wound, given me an ointment for it, and wrapped a bandage around my arm. Then he'd personally made me a hot tea, and we'd found an assortment of old biscuits in his pantry. The cook had also left some stew near the fire.

It was shocking to see how bare some of his pantry shelves were, and how little used his kitchens looked. He'd admitted to only having one cook and one maid in the entire tower, as he rarely had need for more.

We're quite full after having a hot vegetable stew, but we brought a snack with us. A plate of sliced fruit lays between us as we sit and look out at the landscape, marveling at the setting sun slowly transforming the light to dark. I feel like I've entered an entirely new world.

I point at a notable building in the town, built directly into a steep cliff face. "Is that the royal palace? It looks just like the paintings I've seen."

"That's right," he says, swallowing a bite of melon. "No one has lived there for years. I used to advocate that the palace be a living space for people in town, but those above me would never dream of turning the sacred palace into housing."

"I can understand why you would struggle to be heard about that." I've had enough of my own struggles trying to make positive changes to my city.

He points again at the palace. "That's where Queen Morgane first slept when she came to the Oathlands. Back before there were any structures or a name for the land."

"I don't know who that is," I admit.

There is some sadness to his slow nod. "Your Kingdom records have struck Morgane from history, as though she never existed. I may tell you about her sometime, but the hour is getting late, and it's a long story. One I'm afraid you won't like."

"Well, if it's another one of your filthy lies and blemishes against my beloved Kingdom..." I say with a half-smile.

He returns the smile. "Have some fruit so you can shut that mouth up," he says, almost playfully.

"Hey," I say, lightly slapping his shoulder as I laugh.

Things have changed between us since he'd rescued me from those thugs in town. I can see that now. We've both dropped some barriers and there is a comfort and familiarity between us. I don't think there is any fear of clashing or one of us bursting into anger at any point. I can feel the peaceful calm over us like a warm blanket.

Lord Bearon has quietened, and I look over to see a troubled look on him, his brows furrowed.

"You shouldn't have been in town on your own," he says in a low voice. "Anything could have happened to you."

"I wasn't alone. It was just...unfortunate that your guards had lost sight of me for a moment."

He frowns deeply. "I will double the guards on you. At all times."

"Please, no. That is unnecessary. They crowd me enough as it is. I can't have them smothering me. I won't have a moment to myself."

"Is it not more important you're safe, Clio?"

The sound of my name on his lips nearly makes me shiver, but I fight against the urge and instead shake my head. "I don't care if I'm *safer*. You said I had freedom here, and I wish to *feel* that freedom. I can't do that if

I have countless shadows watching my every move, Lord Bearon."

"You can't do that if you're dead, either," he counters.

I blow out a breath, exasperated, though I'm unable to help the warmth that settles around my heart at the quiet concern in his words. It's enough for me to yield just the slightest bit. "Be reasonable, at the very least."

He studies me for a long moment, and eventually nods. "I can add two guards. Two good men. And I will be sure they keep their distance and stay out of sight for the most part. But to have eyes on you at all times."

I smile at him, though it feels strained and sad. "What a terrible burden I must be. If only you could let me go."

His dark eyes meet mine. Curiosity flickers in them. "Do you want to leave?"

"Of course," I say quickly, but there is something in my voice that tells us both I don't fully believe that.

The doubt takes me by surprise. *No, of course I want to leave. Why would I want to stay? But... why does it feel wrong to want to leave?*

I don't press the matter, because I don't want to see if he'd really let me go. It's strange that I no longer have that drive to escape. I hadn't even noticed it was gone until this moment.

"How did you find me so quickly earlier?" I ask. "If your guards had lost sight of me."

For the first time, I see what his guilty expression looks like and it almost makes me smile.

"I may have been following you. Once I learned you had left the tower grounds."

"I see," I say, not minding the idea of him being close by.

"Are you sure you're okay?" he asks, nodding at my bandaged forearm.

"Yes, thank you. It doesn't hurt." Well, it is stinging a little, but I don't want to bother him with that detail. I turn to him and try to decipher what's going on behind his stern, brooding expression. "Why do you care so much? Why are you... being so nice to me?"

His eyes bore into me, and for a long moment we share a lingering look. He has no response to that.

I force myself to look away. Clearing my throat, I say, "There is something I've been meaning to ask, actually. Who was that young girl I saw in your library yesterday?"

"Ah," he says, picking up a piece of fruit. "That's May. My niece."

"Oh. Niece. I thought she was maybe your..."

Lord Bearon does not need me to finish my sentence. He shakes his head. "Never had children."

"And does your niece often spend time in your castle all alone?"

"She does, actually." His voice hardens, telling me this is a difficult subject for him. "May doesn't get on well with her father, Rourk, my brother. She is currently studying history and philosophy, and spends most of her time in the library these days. She's been staying in the tower for almost a year."

"Oh, wow. That must be hard on her and her father to be apart like that."

"That tells me you are close with your father."

I nod. "I miss him, dearly. I think I've grown to look after him too much, even though he doesn't need looking after and he's often too stubborn to accept my support."

"You? Having a stubborn father? I can't imagine that, given your open-minded manner."

I shoot him a wicked glare that just makes him grin.

"Does anyone else live in your tower?" I ask.

"Just my staff." He must see the question about to leave my lips and answers before I can ask. "I have about twenty-three people working for me, to the best of my knowledge. But I have a head groundskeeper who takes care of the staff, so there may be more or less than that."

"More or fewer," I correct.

"Yes, of course. I'm sorry we don't have the fanciest colleges in the land, like your Kingdom," he says sarcastically.

"Twenty-three. That's a lot of people to serve just one person. You must be very important."

He shrugs a massive shoulder. "They tend to the tower, mostly, to keep it upright. My brother hired more guards than I cared for to look over me and the tower."

"It's like this is your royal palace. More than the empty one down there."

"The history of this tower is long and boring," he says. "No one knows its true origin, however. This was here long before Queen Morgane wandered into what would become the Oathlands. The legends say she arrived at night and camped at the foot of the cliff down there, and didn't see this tower until the morning. She lived here for a time but considered it too open to attacks, and so eventually built her palace down where she could be closer to her people."

While I pick at some of the fruit, I notice a silence has come over us. I turn to see him quietly smiling at me.

"I was just thinking..." he says. "I haven't spoken this easily and openly with anyone for a very long time."

"Well, if I may begrudgingly say. I've also noticed how easy you are to talk to. Despite your bull-headedness."

He gives me a '*Me? What about you?*' look, but has the good grace not to voice that.

"No need to worry, Clio," he says. "This doesn't mean we're friends now. I would never dream of such a thing."

"We would be the first Kingdom folk and Oathlander to be friends in hundreds of years."

"The world is a baffling place. Anything is possible."

Something passes over his eyes. I can see he has something he wants to say.

"I also think it's funny," he eventually says, "how we both hold the weight of our kingdoms on our shoulders. We are more alike–"

"Lord Bearon, if you give another example of how the Kingdom and Oathlands are more similar than I think, I may have to slap you."

He laughs heartily at that. It's a throaty, earnest laugh that I find warms me up inside. He is usually so broody that it's nice to see him laugh.

"Please, call me Arthur."

I don't know why, but the way he says this feels full of emotion. Like it is saying more than just the words.

"Arthur. Very well." Suddenly feeling shy, I look away from his piercing gaze.

He picks at the fruit, and as he does so, he shifts his position so he's a little closer to me. "What would you plant in your fields?"

I give him a blank, questioning look.

"You mentioned you had a desire to plant fields and crops. During our stroll through the gardens."

"You remember that?" I say in surprise.

"I meant it when I said I wanted to learn all about you."

His words make me smile, but in the back of my mind I can't help but still feel like he's pretending to be so nice for some nefarious reason.

"Well. Arthur. Fruits and vegetables as standard. I love strawberries. And potatoes. I have in mind a long shelf with potted herb plants. In my vision, I have the less fortunate and homeless tending to my fields, and I'm paying them a wage for their services. That would hopefully give them a sense of purpose and a chance to support themselves again. I've found that usually works better than simply handing them money."

He's watching me and listening intently. "You would eventually need more housing to get people off the streets. You should look into turning some land into housing complexes. You'd need more hands to build those complexes, too. You can even have people teach the less fortunate how to build their own houses."

"I was... actually, yes. That's along the lines of what I've been thinking, long term." I want to ask if he's able to read minds. Is it possible for two people to have such a similar mindset?

"Well," he says, "I guess the Kingdom folk and Oathlanders are more similar than you thought." He braces himself with a protective arm in front of him.

I laugh instead of slapping him. I hadn't realized how funny he could be.

"I'll give you a pass on that one, Lord Be—Arthur."

He nods appreciatively.

"I know nothing about building houses, though," I admit.

"My parents and grandparents built many houses in their time. Between them, they helped build almost a quarter of the entire town. My father was a fair man, but he was too good-hearted. He would always strive to see the good in people, even when they were against him."

Arthur's voice lowers with melancholy, but he doesn't stop speaking. "Growing up, I told myself I wouldn't be like my father. I was going to be strong and live in reality. Not in the ideal world my father thought he lived in. However, as I get older, I realize how great of a man my father truly was. To be that good in a world that supported the cruel and unjust. It made me realize how much I wanted to make the world the kind of place my father saw it to be."

I'm left speechless at how much he's opening up to me, and how sincere he sounds.

A breeze blows over us, washing his spicy cologne over me. It feels like a source of familiar comfort. Like it's bringing back fond childhood memories. I can't stop staring at him, and can't help but notice how easy it has been to talk to him, compared to how little talking I even had the chance to do when I was back home, with my fiance. He was always somewhere else. But Lord Bearon always seems to be right there when I need him. Always seems to know what to say.

Speaking to Lord Bearon... Arthur... isn't anything like speaking to Leonas. It's becoming clear to me how much I've been kidding myself with the engagement. How I've been forcing myself into what I thought was love, simply to make the reality of my arranged marriage something happier than what it was, something that I could convince myself not to despise.

It wasn't the most difficult thing to do, of course; Leonas was not a bad man, even if he had been more distant as of late. He was certainly a beautiful one, too. But I don't think I've ever been so attracted to a man before as I am when I look at Arthur.

And it's because I'm looking at him that I notice the slight bruising on his knuckles.

"Does it hurt?" I ask, feeling bold enough to reach out and lift his large hand.

"It doesn't," he says in a stiff voice that tells me how uncomfortable he is, and how much of a lie those words are. I go to drop his hand, but he simply tightens his fingers around mine, a silent plea for me to not let go.

So I don't.

"Did I thank you? For saving me?" I ask quietly.

We've inched closer during our talking, and our shoulders are touching now. He's much closer than I realized, and I can feel myself slowly drawing closer to him, falling into his dark eyes... towards his full lips.

"You never... need to thank me," he whispers, leaning closer.

His eyes are so sorrowful and powerful.

An overwhelming desire takes over and I cover the distance between us, as though it's the most natural thing to do. Our lips meet, gently at first, as if we might burn each other. Then we kiss passionately as he draws me closer, wrapping an arm around me. His lips are soft as he brings them against mine again and again.

Arthur's fingers trail along my waist, and even through the fabric of my clothing, I feel the heat of his touch. His tongue gently teases at the seam of my lips, and it takes only the slightest bit of encouragement from him for me to open to him, letting his tongue sweep into my mouth.

He tastes of melon, of warm spring days and cool breezes, of summer prairies in the light of the moon.

Arthur suddenly pulls away, shocking me. He has a troubled, guilty look on his face, and I know instantly he regrets his actions. Why was I stupid enough to kiss him? I still don't know what came over me.

"I'm sorry, I..." I begin, but don't know what to say.

A deafening horn blares in the air, startling us both.

Arthur jumps to his feet. Before I can ask what the horn means, he says, "We are under attack."

My heart leaps into my throat. Attack? Does that mean... my Kingdom folk are here?

"Go inside and stay there," he says. "I want you here *safe*, Clio. I mean it."

With that, he steps to the edge of the roof and leaps off, falling from sight.

Chapter Twenty

ARTHUR

I make my way through town the fastest way I know how—across the rooftops. The golden light has faded enough from the day that I'm not at risk of being seen clearly. Anyone would just see a figure bounding across the roofs.

After entering the military compound to find my brother, I'm told he has gone to the West Farm Gate with a platoon of soldiers. So I rush off to catch them before they leave town.

The horn is a call to arms, signaling an impending attack on our people. It's a sound I've heard only twice before in my life, and each time it has sent my heart spiraling.

My mind is already spinning from the kiss I'd just shared with Clio. What had we been thinking? I can almost guarantee that neither of us were thinking clearly. And she must think terribly of me for pulling away from the kiss. How can I begin to tell her why I pulled away? She'd never understand. But I can't dwell on that right now.

I leap off a barn rooftop and land near the group of soldiers on the edge of town, my shoulders heaving with my panting breath. I remind myself to keep up with my regular physical training, which I've been neglecting lately. An ordinary man would not have been able to cover the distance I've just covered without stopping. But I am no ordinary man.

Rourk is among the thirty or so soldiers heading out into the farmland beyond town. The last rays of light are being swallowed by the darkness as I reach him. In this part of town with little light, the sky overhead is already filled with stars. The clinking of the soldier's armor is the only sound in the quiet night.

Rourk sees me approaching and stops to face me. He doesn't seem surprised to see me.

"We have unknowns spotted in the nearby woods, scouting the area," Rourk says. It's rare to see him in the full combat armor of the General Commander, which gives him an impressively large silhouette.

"The Kingdom?" I ask.

He shakes his head. "We're not sure yet, but they're coming from that direction, and they don't seem like Wildmen." The look in his eyes tells me he is sure it's Kingdom scouts, and that I'm the reason they're here.

I notice some soldiers gathered nearby were part of the group I'd taken to the Kingdom. Their awkwardness and nerves around me is clear, and they avoid eye contact with me. I've disgraced all those who followed me into enemy territory. We were meant to have been heroes.

"Let's go," I say.

Rourk holds a hand up to stop me. "Arthur. I can't have you accompanying us. The Grandmaster General is out for your blood as it is. I know you want to help, but you're a civilian. And we don't have time to argue this."

"You're right, we don't have time," I say, stepping forward. "Right now, you need all the help you can get. Tell me you don't prefer to have me out there, watching your backs."

Rourk sighs and shakes his head in defeat. "You were never here," he says as he begins leading his men forward. "Is that understood?" he yells to the others.

Cries of 'yes sir' ripple through them.

We head out into the darkness, leaving the warm lights of the town behind us. The shapes of distant trees are just visible, but I don't need light to know the land around us. The land I grew up in.

My mind races with chaotic thoughts as we make our way towards the woods, staying close to a row of rocks that form a wall.

Along with that kiss just a moment ago, I can't stop thinking about my findings yesterday. The true meaning of Clio's birthmark. I've yet to figure out how I'm going to tell her. How can I even begin to explain the truth to her? I haven't even fully decided if I ever will tell her.

No, that's not true. I will tell her, of course.

She has a right to know who she really is.

The unease among the soldiers is almost palpable in the air. It's been a long while since many of them have seen any kind of battle outside of training.

I hear one soldier whisper to another, "What's he doing here? He's not even armed."

The soldiers that know me are aware of how I can help. But I'm sure it must look odd to have this Lord with them in a fine shirt and trousers, with no weapon or armor. The rest of them are carrying swords or spears, have knives on their belts, and some have small round shields attached to their left forearms.

The other soldier, who is familiar with me, whispers back. "You haven't seen anything yet."

I could request a sword, as I'm well-trained with them, but I've found that my preference is to fight unarmed. It's been a very long time since I've fought to kill as many opponents as I can, and I don't intend to kill anyone tonight.

By the time we reach the edge of the woods, we can hear the soft rustling of leaves ahead. Someone is walking around nearby, though we can't see them yet. Rourk signals for his men to fan out. He has trained them for combat in the woods, at least, as it's a likely location for battling invading forces.

Rourk meets my eyes, and he points up. I nod and leap up onto a thick branch, disappearing from their view. I climb higher and make my way between the trees, carefully picking the right branches to guide my path. I have the wrong shoes on for the grip I need, but I'll make do.

The sounds of people moving through the undergrowth below reach me when I stop and listen, but I can tell from the rustling of armor that they're my soldiers. I'll need to urge Rourk to train them to be quieter.

There is enough moonlight and starlight to see glints of movement through the dimness of the trees, although there are too many thick clouds for my liking.

I jump to the next tree and hug the trunk, supporting myself with one foot on a branch. Easing forward for a better view, I see the approaching enemy below. Beneath their weathered cloaks is the white gleam of their padded armor. King's Guard.

The Kingdom really has come into the Oathlands.

There are only three of them, as far as I can see, and something is telling me these are not part of a larger army. If there was a battalion of enemy soldiers out there, they'd be coming in force, not sending a few out here. No, these are simply scouts. And that means they might not even be looking for trouble. They could just be in search of Clio, thinking she might be lost in the wilderness. But why would they come so close to our borders?

One of the enemy scouts picks up his pace, likely having heard our approaching soldiers. To the side, I hear the first break-out of fighting as someone cries out and swords clash.

No way to avoid the fight now.

I leap down and crash into an enemy scout, grabbing his sword and throwing it away into the darkness. He pushes himself to his feet and tries to tackle me, but I wrap my arms around him and haul him off his feet. He's thrown several feet through the air and slams into a tree trunk, tumbling to the ground.

That alerts another scout to my presence. He comes rushing out from the darkness with his sword drawn. I catch his attacking arm and my elbow flashes to crack his jaw.

Two more enemy scouts break through the foliage as I hear my soldiers making their way toward us. The sounds of fights all around tell me I've underestimated how many scouts there are.

I thrust a foot against my attacker, knocking him down, and leap up to disappear into the trees. I'm more useful up here. Making my way to two scouts below, fear grips my heart. Not fear for my safety. Fear that these men will take Clio away from me. I know I cannot keep her held against her will forever, but it feels like we've only just begun to really see each other. And I don't want that to end.

I drop onto the two scouts, throwing them to the ground. One of my soldiers comes and drives his sword through the chest of one of the downed scouts before I can stop him. But it's too late. The scout blows out his last breath as blood pools out of his mouth.

There's no way these soldiers would understand my desire to not shed any more blood tonight. Even though a part of me knows there is no good outcome to letting any of these scouts live.

I rush about with the soldiers, doing what I can to keep my men protected. I use my strengths to overpower the enemy and surprise attack them from above, leaping from tree to tree without being seen.

The enemy is soon defeated, with many of them killed.

Rourk is unscathed, save for being muddied and splatters of blood from both friend and foe on his armor.

He calls out for the soldiers to look for more scouts, to start gathering numbers of casualties, already planning, ordering, *leading*.

This is the way between Kingdom and Oathlands. The way it has always been. If anyone enters enemy territory, it means their lives are forfeit.

So why did I not want to shed any blood tonight?

Rourk comes to me, his eyes alive with murder and adrenaline. "I fear war is imminent, brother. This is just the start. If there is another great war, we will not survive."

"What do you propose?"

He swallows. "We must flee. Leave our land. Or risk being slaughtered."

The idea of an entire town running into the wilderness unsettles my stomach.

"If we run, we're going to be running for the rest of our lives," I tell him.

I have no idea what we're going to do next. But I know one thing.

This is all my fault.

Chapter Twenty-One

CLIO

The next morning brings with it another chance to explore the town. I don't know how much longer I'm going to be here, but I refuse to simply wait to be rescued.

And... if I'm being completely honest with myself, I'm not sure how much I want to be rescued anymore. Not right away, anyway. But at the very least, I want to learn more about the Oathlands and see what an escape route would look like if it came to that.

Perhaps, after all of this, I might be able to restore the relationship between the Kingdom of Aer and the Oathlands. Maybe we can be the allies we once were, ages ago.

I'm not quite ready to face Arthur again, so spending the day in town sounds good to me. I feel like an idiot for kissing him, and all I can think about is how he pulled away. Maybe he feels sorry for me. Maybe this is all part of his master manipulation plan. I have no idea anymore.

As if swept up in my wake, the more I walk, the more I seem to collect guards. I pass down the hall and see a familiar guard standing at attention.

"Good morning, Felix," I say with a nod.

"Good morning, my lady," he says cheerily. "If it pleases you, I would like to join your band of merry followers this morning."

"Join in," I say, looking back as I keep walking. "The more the merrier. If I see you in town, I'll buy you a treat from the bakery."

He smiles broadly and thanks me.

As part of keeping me comfortable during my stay here, Lord Bearon—Arthur, I mean. I must remember to call him Arthur—has provided me with a pouch of coins to spend as I wish. It isn't much, especially compared to what I'm used to carrying in the Kingdom, but I've been told that items are much cheaper in the Oathlands, so I shouldn't need much to get by.

My mind drifts to my meeting with Arthur late last night, when he'd returned to me. The horn had been a false alarm and there had been no attack on the town. That had come as a mix of relief and disappointment. Relief that no one I knew had been hurt, and disappointment that there was no rescue attempt.

Does that mean my Kingdom does not know where I am? Perhaps they have already announced me dead or have given up their search, despite me being gone for less than a week.

There had been a moment last night when I thought Arthur and I would kiss again. A look in his eyes and a tense silence between us. But neither of us had brought up that initial kiss. It was as though it had never happened.

I truly don't know what to think anymore. I can't believe I kissed someone who is not my fiance, arranged marriage or no. More than that, though, I can't believe I actually kissed an *Oathlander*. But Arthur is unlike anyone I've ever met. It feels like I can see directly into his good heart.

The more I think about him, the more I see how Leonas and I have never been right for each other. He's never made me feel even half of what I feel when I'm with Arthur. But that just makes me feel bad for Leonas. Sweet, kind, thoughtful Leonas.

Stop getting ahead of yourself, you silly girl. I shake my head as I leave the tower, heading into the front gardens. A part of me knows I'll be back home someday. Back in the arms of Leonas. Then I can put all this foolishness behind me.

I shouldn't be thinking of Lord Bearon so much. For all I know, he really has been trying to seduce me for some wicked purpose.

As I reach the front gate, I see that young girl, May, strolling around the inner wall. She catches sight of me and straightens.

I nod and bid her a good morning. "Out for a morning stroll?"

"I find a morning walk, and some sunshine, helps clear my head for studying," she says.

Now that I see her better, I can see some family resemblance with her and Arthur. Similar sharp cheekbones and the shape of the eyes. Although May's hair is much fairer than Arthur's full black and her eyes are blue.

I want to ask why she isn't living with her father, but I don't want to pry. Especially when I don't even know the girl.

May eyes me thoughtfully. "I've heard about you. You're Clio, right? My uncle's special guest."

"Special guest?" I ask, raising a brow.

"Well, the guards and other staff have said little, but they've seen you around the castle. Don't worry, I don't care much for gossip and I have no intention of snooping around my uncle's affairs."

"You are wise beyond your years," I tell her.

She holds out her hand. "I should be going, anyway. But it's nice to meet you again, Clio."

I shake her hand and tell her the pleasure is mine. Something in her eyes gives me pause. May seems to stiffen, her features hardening and brows crinkling, like she's in pain. Then she snaps out of it as our hands part and she's back to her casual, cheery self.

I watch her walk into the tower and wonder what had just happened. She seems just as odd as her uncle. It makes me wonder what her father is like, though I'm not so sure I wish to learn the answer to that question.

I don't mind the walk into town so much today. Perhaps I'm getting used to all the walking I've been doing lately. And it could be that I have prepared better with more comfortable shoes today, which match my brown flowing dress. The garment is a little frumpy for my tastes, but it fits me well, at least.

When I leave the declining mountainous pathways, I take a different route into town. Looking back, I can see three of the six guards in view.

I come to a wide cobbled street and see children playing a game where one throws a ball up as high as they can, and the others have to try to catch it after one bounce. The sounds of innocent, childish laughter brings a smile to my face. I can smell fresh bread from somewhere nearby, which makes my stomach grumble.

A square is ahead, with an unused water fountain in the center. I'm struck by how similar this square is to a place in the Kingdom, near the castle. Same layout, same roads that lead away from it, and even a similar water fountain feature. I wonder if that is a coincidence or somehow intentional.

I pass by old women knitting and quietly chatting. Their easy-going, carefree lives bring me comfort. It reminds me that these Oathlanders are just regular people like me. They don't seem to mind their simple, somewhat tattered clothing. I suppose it matches their simple lives. But they seem so happy.

A few minutes later, I reach a short bridge that crosses into the next section of town. A deep crevasse is cutting through the ground, about ten feet wide where the bridge is, and there are railings and fences running along the edge to stop anyone from falling in.

It's a wonder to me how the land and the town are combined as one. I'm not used to so many levels and layers to a place, and it makes me realize just how flat and boring the Kingdom is, save for its sky-piercing structures. The Oathlands has none of the extravagance of the Kingdom, but it has a quiet grace and, possibly, even more wonder to it.

The faint sound of music is carrying on the wind, though I can't see where it's coming from.

I climb up a short set of stairs and come to a winding road that seems popular with many people. One thing I've noticed is that the Oathlands has a lot of stairs, either made of wood or carved into the ground. Some as few as three steps to help people go up a rocky path.

A young woman with bright eyes, perhaps a few years younger than me, approaches with a nervous smile.

"Excuse me. You are the woman seen walking with Lord Bearon?" There is a husky undertone to her light, youthful voice.

"I... suppose I am. Yes," I tell her, not seeing any reason to lie.

An older man with a mustache overhears and perks up. He steps away from the cart of wooden blocks he's been pushing and wipes his hands as he says, "So you're the reason we've been seeing so much of Lord Bearon these days?"

"So much of him?" I ask, noticing our talk has drawn a few eyes on us in the street.

The older man chuckles. "I've seen him more times in the last few days than I have in the last few months."

A middle-aged couple walking by come to a stop next to us.

"Lord Bearon was here? Where?" the woman asks, looking around.

"He's not here," the young woman says. "But I saw him, too. I've always thought he spends too much time up in his tower."

"He's the most mysterious man I've ever known," the mustached man says. "Tell you the truth, I don't trust him. Can't trust a man who doesn't enjoy being around his people."

"Of course he likes us," the young woman says, as if personally offended. "After all he's done for us, how can he not like us?"

The woman of the couple says, "I won't have a word said against him. He's the reason we're not under the Kingdom's rule."

"Our guardian eats here for free," someone from a sandwich hut calls out.

I ask my nearest companions, "I've heard some call him Fireheart. Why is that?"

The young woman's eyes light up. I can see she is quite taken by Lord Bearon. I imagine many women in town are.

"It's because his heart is full of fire. Passion," she says. "Full of fire for his people. They say that fire keeps us safe and warm, and also burns our enemies."

The man of the couple mutters, "I always thought it's because he has bad indigestion."

The woman beside him elbows him.

"Anyway, I must be going," the young woman says. "I just wanted to say thank you for bringing our lord back to us. I've never seen him smile so much. And he deserves it. Always looking so broody, like he's about to cry. Oh, please don't tell him I think he cries."

"I won't. I promise," I say, and wish the small crowd a good day as I continue walking. Everyone seems so friendly and easy to talk to.

It's interesting to hear more about how the people view Lord Bearon. The mysterious recluse up in his tower. Their guardian. I wonder if any of them has seen even half of the real man I've come to know.

Perhaps Arthur is like me. People only see what they want to see from him. He is whoever they want him to be. It matters little who he really is.

The musical sound of flutes and violins grows louder, and it isn't long before I come to a grassy area where a circle of women are dancing. It almost looks like a festival of some kind. Some people gather around the grassy center of the area, clapping and cheering. The air is alive with merriment and good humor.

I stop to admire the dancing, which is a little similar to a dance I know, but with a faster rhythm, and this one seems more vigorous. The long skirts of the dancing women ripple and flare about them. They're all wearing matching white blouses with a blue flower design, and black skirts adorned with gold leaves.

The dancing women move in a circle with a small gap between the first and last, and when they come close to where I'm standing, one of them reaches out and encourages me to join them.

I try to decline the offer but it's clear there is no use, and the woman gets me to join the end of their circle. I can't help but laugh as I try to keep up with them dancing, holding hands with the woman beside me. The crowd cheers louder at my addition. The steps are fairly simple, once I focus enough to follow along, but now and then they throw in a twirl or a quick duck down that throws me off.

When a young boy comes up to us, I almost knock into him, before I manage to stop and see what he wants. He waves at me to bend down and holds up a wreath of vibrant flowers and leaves. I crouch low enough to allow him to place the wreath on my head.

"Thank you very much," I say.

The boy giggles and runs back into the crowd. I continue dancing with the merry ladies, getting caught up in the festivities. The music is playful and fun, and the people around me are having the best time, as though they have not a care in the world.

This is what I've been looking for, I realize. A genuine look at who these people are. The kind, gentle, loving Oathlanders. They are good-hearted people just trying to live.

Sure, there are those who would threaten to rob and assault me, and the town has similar issues with the homeless as we do back home, but every large body of people has their problems. And those problems do not speak for the vast majority.

These people may be living a more urban life, and don't seem to mind the dirt smudges, worn clothes, unkempt hair, and basic amenities, but I can appreciate their carefree, relaxed way of life. I'm too used to people dressing to impress, wearing expensive jewelry and gossiping about who has the better life.

I'm laughing as the music ends and the women stop to bow at the applause from the crowd. I bow with them and they point and cheer at me especially. I thank them for the dance and manage to leave before they drag me back to the circle. The next song begins as I walk away, still chuckling at how much fun I've just had.

Ahead, I recognize a familiar face.

Chapter Twenty-Two

CLIO

I've spotted that old man who had given me the crystal. He's walking down the street with a teenage boy I haven't seen before.

The old man is bent with age and walks with a stick to support him, while the boy also supports him with a hand on his elbow. While the boy can't be over sixteen, he stands a foot taller than the bent old man.

"I've been looking for you," I say as I approach them.

The old man looks up with a tense face, concentrating on his walking, but he relaxes and his eyes widen when he recognizes me.

"Oh ho! There you are, young lady. I was wondering when I'd see you again." He has a surprisingly light voice for an old man, although there is an undercurrent of gravel and frailty.

I glance at the young boy and say to the man, "Is now a good time to talk?"

"Yes, yes. This is my youngest grandson, Elias. He's the good one," he chuckles. "Elias, my boy, why don't you fetch us some iced juice from that stall I like? You know the one. My friend and I will sit over on that bench and wait for you."

The boy seems uncertain, especially when he looks at me, but the old man insists that he does what he says.

"So stubborn," he says as we watch the boy leave. "He gets that from his mother, gods be good to her."

I take the arm of the old man and help him sit on a wooden bench on the side of the road. I wipe away a sheen of sweat on my forehead from all the dancing and smooth out my dress.

He turns to me. "Nice head ornament."

I remember the wreath on my head and take it off, and play with it absently in my hands.

"You have not told me your name," the old man says.

"And you haven't told me yours. I am Clio."

"Clio what?"

I eye him suspiciously. "Clio Welling."

He huffs as though he doesn't believe me, and I have to wonder if I'm a terrible liar.

"Well, Clio, my name is Ecosar. Ecosar Odren. But, I am not the important one here. Ayyoo?"

The strange sound comes out with glee, and I can see anticipation in his large eyes and crooked smile.

"Ah, yes, well... I... I saw the light in the crystal." I don't tell him about the light that had flashed and scared away that red-eyed beast. "Mind telling me what it means?"

He's practically giddy, like I'm telling him he's just won a large fortune.

"I've waited a long time for this day, let me tell you. Now, have you heard of the Fae?"

"The... fairy people from the old stories?" I ask, sounding confused. I hadn't expected our discussion to go this route. From his expectant look, I see I'm meant to keep talking. "They are like fairies, but the size of regular folk, with large petal-like wings, who could grant wishes."

"Some of that is true, aye. They did not have wings and they did not grant wishes, so to speak. But they were magical and, in a way, they could grant you gifts. You see, they could bring out and enhance the magic of those around them."

I struggle to follow exactly why we're having this conversation, and what this has to do with the crystal, but I nod and listen.

"Long ago," Ecosar begins, "the Oathlands was a land full of magic and wonder. But, once the Fae were all slain, that magic was lost. It was so long ago that many today only think of them as stories. But I know them to be true. And there hasn't been a Fae in these parts for a very long time."

"Okay," I say. "That's interesting and all, but I have to ask what this has to do with the crystal."

"There hasn't been a Fae in these parts for a very long time," he says again, and adds, "until now."

A shiver washes over me. I don't like the intense way he's staring at me.

"I wonder if your Fae blood has been passed down through the generations, laying dormant and somehow awakened upon your birth. Or perhaps a significant moment in your life awakened the Fae in you. Magic has always infuriatingly worked in mysterious ways."

I swallow through my dry throat. "Excuse me. I'm sorry. What are you saying, exactly?"

"Only a Fae could summon the light from the crystal." His light voice has become eerie now, the gravelly quality becoming more pronounced. "Your hair, bright red, is the color of a Fae's hair. Yes, these days there are those with red hair who are ordinary folk. But, sometimes, I wonder if the red-haired folk are descendants of the Fae. In your case, I was finally proven right."

"Sir, you must be mistaken," I say with some authority. "I was not born in the Oathlands–"

"Ah," he says. "You were born in the Kingdom."

My breath catches and I freeze.

"Not to worry, dear Clio. I will not tell a soul."

"How did you...?" I ask in awe.

"You have a way about you that reminds me of your people."

An Oathlander who is familiar with the Kingdom folk? That sounds like a story I'd like to hear. But I have more important things on my mind.

"So, you see, it isn't possible for me to have Fae blood, as you claim. I was born in the Kingdom. Our blood has never mixed with anyone outside of our land. Everyone knows the Fae have never ventured into the city."

He chuckles and ends up having a small coughing fit. Once he recovers, he says, "What a foolish thing to say. Our lands have always shared blood."

That can't be true. Can it? I'm finding it hard to know what to think anymore.

"Allow me to help you, dear gentle soul," he says. "I have a series of breathing exercises for you to help connect to and channel your magic. Please, keep the crystal for now and practice channeling your light through it."

We spend some time going through the exercises. They seem simple enough. The hard part is having to clear my mind of all thoughts and to really focus on my breathing. It takes me a while to get the hang of what he wants from me.

I still don't fully understand everything he's been saying, but I have a feeling in the pit of my stomach that I should be listening to him.

"You seem to know so much," I say once we take a break from the breathing. "What do you know of the history of wars between our lands."

His eyes narrow in thought. "You should find a book. It can be found in a library in town. It will tell you what you're looking for."

"And I should believe whatever I read in a book?"

"Not all books, perhaps. But this one, yes. For it tells the full truth you're looking for. You won't find this book anywhere close to the Kingdom as all other copies have been burned or lost through time."

"Can you tell me anything yourself?"

He sucks on the inside of his cheek. "How about this for trivia you won't hear often. The King of the Kingdom and the First Queen of the Oathlands were once married."

A laugh bursts from me. "That's ridiculous."

He doesn't share my laugh. "After many disagreements, the Queen left the Kingdom and took some loyal followers with her. Some time after she settled in what would become the Oathlands, your King went out with his men and murdered the Queen. That is how the wars began between our people. History says the Oathlanders were the first to attack. But that attack was a retaliation for the murder of their Queen."

My head feels heavy, and my vision is spinning.

He gives me the name of the book and points me in the direction of the library.

Chapter Twenty-Three

ARTHUR

The sounds of battle ring out all around me. I watch as the soldiers spar. Swords clash and boots shuffle in the dirt, while other men run drills and physical challenges about the training grounds. They're going through sword attack combinations and defensive maneuvers, throwing knives and axes at target boards, and wrestling in pairs in the sparring circle. They are doing everything right, and yet, I know it will not be enough if the Kingdom attacks.

Rourk and the Grandmaster General have been too lax with their training. They're not pushing the soldiers enough. Only a handful of our soldiers have seen actual combat against an enemy, so their lack of experience or fortitude is not entirely their fault. But I, as someone who has seen my share of battles and known many deaths, know what it truly takes to survive.

I don't see that killer instinct in the men training before me. I still don't really know why I've come here today. Is it that I don't trust myself being around Clio right now? My mind has been a maelstrom ever since our kiss. Perhaps I'm just trying to distract myself.

I search for Rourk around the grounds, thinking I can ask him to lunch if he hasn't eaten yet. Spending time with my brother would be a good distraction.

As if summoned by my thoughts, I spot Rourk walking across the training grounds, coming towards me. His gait is strong and there is bloody murder in his eyes, which gets my guard up.

Rourk reaches me and points a finger. "Just when in the hells were you going to tell me about your prisoner?" His tone is hot and challenging, and his shoulders are heaving with his restrained anger.

My body's instinctual reaction is to freeze, but I can't. Not if I want to play it cool, casual, show no guilt or acknowledgement of wrongdoing. That sort of thing has only ever made Rourk angrier. "I was going to tell you," I say, "when things had cooled down here. I didn't want to give you more to worry about than you already had on your plate." My mind is spinning, trying to figure out who might have told him about who—what—Clio is. Who else knows?

"Don't put this on me," he says, seething. "This was all you." He steps us both to the side, away from the sparring soldiers. "Speak the truth, brother. Are you trying to start a war?"

"No. Of course not."

"Then why do you have the niece of King De'Kalo locked up in your castle?"

My chest tightens and my voice leaves me. I suddenly feel light-headed. The niece of the king? Clio? I feel like I've just been slapped.

"What are you talking about?" I ask.

"I'm talking about *you*, brother, kidnapping a member of their royal family. What were you thinking?"

Clio. A princess.

"I... didn't know," I manage to say, feeling the need to steady myself. "She... she told me she was the daughter of a cook. I..."

"You weren't thinking, that's what."

"How do you...?"

Rourk eyes me sternly, his jaw clenching the way it does when he becomes defensive. "Some of my men finally saw fit to tell me of the prisoner you'd taken from the Kingdom."

"But... how do you know who she is?" I search his eyes for the truth.

"That is not relevant. What is of the utmost relevance is what we're going to do with her."

"You're mistaken," I quickly say. "You must be. She is not the niece of the King."

"She is. Trust me. She is." His severe look tells me the truth.

It clicks, then. The sincerity of which he says it, the unwavering truth. There are few people he would trust so deeply—himself and his daughter. And May, with those visions she gets... They must have had contact. I suddenly remember the time I found them both in the library, but there was no sign May knew anything. Clio and May must have run into each other again. Perhaps literally, if they touched each other.

Still, I have to make sure I'm right. "May?"

Rourk nods gravely.

I frown and bite back a curse. How could I have let this happen? I should have known there was a chance of Clio and May interacting. My temples burn and throb.

"Wake up and see the light of day, brother," Rourk says.

How could she not have told me? She lied to me. I have to remind myself that I am her captor, and she my captive, so I can't be too surprised that she'd hidden her true self from me. I can't blame her for not fully trusting me. But... why does it sting so much?

I consider telling Rourk about Clio's birthmark. The one that marks her as someone very special. But in his current aggressive state, I don't think it's the right time to say more than I have to.

"I will handle this," I tell him.

"Handle it how? You cannot bring harm to her."

"I wouldn't," I say, too quickly. That gets his attention, and his eyes search me carefully.

"I will not harm her," I add. "I promise you that. Now I know who she really is... allow me time to decide on my actions. I have brought this onto myself. They need not be the problems of the town. No one knows she is here, outside of our borders."

"I hope for your sake that is true," Rourk says, his fists clenched at his side. "Now, go from my sight. I don't want your ineptitude rubbing off on my men any more than it already has."

That cuts me hard. I watch him turn and leave with a lump in my throat. We've clashed many times before, but this feels different. This feels gravely serious. The repercussions of my actions weigh me down and force a long, weary sigh out as I leave the training grounds.

Beyond the grounds, I see one of my uniformed guards idly patrolling the pathway leading up a slope. There's never one of my men too far from me. I get his attention as I walk up to him.

"Gavin. Do you know where Lady Welling is at this moment?"

He nods, standing to attention. "I spoke with Cheston some time ago, my lord. He says they spotted her wandering into the Regent Gardens."

"Very good. As you were." I dismiss him and make my way into town towards the Regent Gardens, heading across a bridge.

Clio is the niece of the king? And she bears that birthmark of Oathlands royalty. What does this all mean? I have to wonder if she's been lying to me this entire time. Had she meant to stow away on our wagon, to enter the Oathlands under the guise of a prisoner?

I curse myself as I head through town. How could I have been so naïve? There is no other way a woman like her could have shown such interest in me. Why else would she have been so understanding and nice towards her captor? She's been plotting against me this entire time.

I find two more of my guards along the way and get better directions from them. I find Clio in a meadow hidden within the Regent Gardens, enclosed from the broader park. Shrubs and foliage surround her, and tall trees let some of the golden sun rays into her secluded meadow.

My heart pounds at the sight of her, resting against a tree with a book in her hands, and her dress pooled around her. The softness of her skin. The creaminess of her legs showing from under her dress. Her full lips part at the sight of me, which makes me ache for her even more. In the sunlight, her hair is as bright as an open flame.

No, stop this. Think with your head for once, I tell myself.

"An interesting read?" I ask, not knowing what else to say.

She shows me the cover. A book about ancient magic and folklore.

"You look like you ran here," she says, watching me closely, yet with a casual air.

My heart is racing, but not from any physical exertion. Am I really in the presence of Kingdom royalty?

Now that I look at her, I see it clearly. Her grace and poise. The stiff posture of her seating position. Her delicate nature. I see it all so blatantly in front of me. It was hard to see before, with her dressed in our homely Oathlands clothes, and her without her meticulously done hair and the jewelry she likely usually wears. The way she spoke to me, when we were first getting to know each other. But now, I can so easily picture her in a ball gown adorned with jewels.

"Arthur?" she questions me with raised brows.

I clear my throat and step closer. "I haven't seen you all day. I wondered if... if perhaps you've been keeping your distance from me."

Her eyes widen briefly before she composes herself. "I... well, perhaps I have been."

"I understand."

She looks up at me. "Do you?"

"I do. You want your freedom. You don't want the constant reminder of seeing your captor."

I sense her deflating a little, though it's subtle. She nods and manages a smile. "You are very perceptive."

I have to wonder if I said the wrong thing. Was she expecting me to say something else?

"Would you come and sit?" she asks, closing the book and laying it beside her.

I do as she asks, settling down beside her. We're surrounded by the serene air of the meadow, filled with chirping birds. It's as though we're enclosed in our own world, away from everyone.

"I've been meaning to ask," she begins, her bright blue eyes watching me. "How is it you were able to leap off your tower in the way you did the other night?"

I grin ruefully, looking away. "I have been training my entire life, on an almost daily basis." That's a variation of the answer I usually give to those who witness my excessive prowess.

Clio cocks her head, unimpressed. "That is not what I witnessed. I saw something... remarkable. Without explanation."

I can see she is distracted and anxious, but I don't know what's really on her mind.

"We both have our secrets," I tell her, feeling bold.

Her eyes flash with shock as she meets my gaze for a second before turning away. I'm not ready to confront her about what I know. I want us to keep up this façade for a little longer—to keep her as the daughter of a cook and me as a simple lord—as I don't know what's going to happen to us once the truth comes out.

"What brought about your interest in that book?" I ask. "That isn't an easy find."

Clio sighs, pausing a moment before shaking her head. I can see she's deciding to tell me something.

She turns back towards me, her eyes now widened with excitement. "I met the old man in town again," she said a bit breathlessly, "and he told me he knew my true identity. He mentioned something about a Fae crystal. I saw a strange light within it, and he told me that meant I had Fae blood running through me." She paused, gauging my reaction. "Can you believe it?"

I'm blindsided as I listen. I know she's truly the niece of King DeKalo, but I hadn't been expecting her to talk about Fae and ancient magic.

"Perhaps you shouldn't listen to every eccentric old man you meet," I grumble.

She reaches into a pocket in her skirt and pulls out a thick blue-hued crystal, now nestled in her palm. "This is a Fae crystal. Well, two people have told me that, anyway."

"Yes, I've heard about them. They were used to enhance magic in the old days. They say that the Fae channeled their magic through them and expanded their magic to others. But those are just stories, Clio. And even if they are true, that was all so long ago. Whatever magic the crystal once held would surely have disappeared by now. Along with the rest of the magic in the world."

"Do you believe the old stories? About magic, and dragons, and witches?"

I shrug and try to appear unconcerned. "They've always been stories to me. I've never actually considered them to be true. I suppose... in the back of my mind, deep down, I've thought of magic as being part of the old world. Something so long ago and so obscure and unfathomable that it doesn't bear thinking about."

I regard her, trying to decipher the person inside. Why is she trying to distract me with all this talk about magic and Fae?

"Can I ask about your mother and father?" I ask.

Her brows rise.

"My... mother and father? Where has this question come from?"

I cock my head casually, as though I'm just making conversation. "I'm curious. Indulge me. I'll let you know if you have any magical heritage."

She gives me a wry smile. "Fine. Well, there isn't much to say, really." Her eyes are alive as she takes a moment. Is she trying to make up a story about her fake parents?

"My mother is a cook in the royal castle. This you know already. And my father was a shepherd at the castle. He grew up working in the fields, as did my mother. That's where they met."

"And your family can be traced back to the Kingdom for many generations?" My question earns me an odd look.

"Well, of course they can. Why would you ask that?"

"The Fae lived in the Oathlands, according to the stories. I've never heard of one coming from the Kingdom before."

She frowns, which makes my heart ache. I only want to see her smiling and laughing. It makes me feel alive inside.

When her deep blue eyes lock onto me, my breath catches.

"Do you really think the old man was wrong about me?" she asks.

"I do. But if you'd like to learn more about the Fae, I have several books about them in my personal library."

That seems to make her feel better. "Thank you, Arthur."

We share a lingering look for so long that I feel myself falling slowly towards her. But I catch myself and sit firmly. She's never looked at me in this way before. I feel like there's a fire burning between us, and neither one of us dares get close enough to burn.

Her eyes flicker down to my lips and back up to meet my gaze, and I know then that she must be thinking of the kiss we shared before, the same as I am. But she sucks in a shaky breath and asks, "I've been here for some time now. I have to wonder, Arthur... what are you going to do with me?"

Her lips look soft and are glistening in the sunlight. Her eyes beckon me closer.

I don't know where the words come from or what part of me summons them from my lips, but I say, "What would you like me to do with you?"

She draws closer, and so do I, covering the minimal yet vast distance between us. I'm overwhelmed at the moment and all I know is my deep hunger for her. I sense her trembling as our lips meet.

We kiss gently first, hesitating. I feel the soft, whispering brush of her lips, fleeting and ethereal. Then our passions take over and we kiss deeper, with force. I settle one hand at the side of her neck and the other in the long waves of red hair that fall down her back, unable to keep from tangling my fingers in it. I tug, just a little, and a breathy moan slips from her lips.

"Fuck," I whisper against her lips. "Answer the question, Clio." I make myself move a little further away. "What would you like me to do to you?"

Her eyes flutter back open, and they're staring into mine as she says, "Everything."

I'm no longer in control of my actions as I lay her down on the grass. I breathe her in as we kiss passionately, losing ourselves in the moment. I slide my tongue against her lips, and then into her mouth when she opens for me, and her legs wrap around my waist. I roll my covered hips against her, and she exhales sharply, the sound a slight pant as she pushes herself against me, desperate for more pressure. I hadn't realized how much I needed to feel her against me, to taste her, to be one with her, until this very moment. How much I craved this.

My hands drift lower, to the skin of her thighs where her skirts have ridden up far enough to let me softly trace my fingers against the smoothness of her body. "Are you sure, Clio?"

She nods. "Yes."

That confirmation has me bringing my hands up higher. I tease them along her damp underwear, just one knuckle lightly brushing against the fabric that covers her. Blood rushes to her cheeks as her head falls back. She squeezes her thighs tighter around me before loosening them again and spreading them further apart, baring herself to me in a far more open way than before.

I hook a finger in her underwear, her slickness immediately on my finger. "You're so wet, Clio," I murmur. "How long have you been like this for me?"

"Please," she whispers, shaking her head.

I don't make her answer, considering it looks like she might not be having the easiest time forming coherent thoughts right now. Instead, I slide her underwear off her body and push her skirts up further, bunching them at her waist as I gaze down at her lean body, flushed with arousal exactly where it matters the most.

I slide two fingers inside her folds and gather her wetness on them, feeling my cock grow to a painful hardness. I ignore it, focusing wholly on her as I bring those fingers up to her clit, coating it in her own wetness as I swirl my fingers around the bud. She cries out softly and her legs fight to close again, but I hold one of them open with my free hand.

"So beautiful. You know that, don't you Clio?"

Her response is a shaky moan as I work my fingers in tighter circles. Wetness trickles from her folds and slides down her thighs. My eyes track the movement, and suddenly my fingers aren't enough.

I drop my mouth onto her, and my tongue is quickly lapping up her dampness. Clio cries out again, her pleasure ringing in my ears. Her hands wind their way into my hair as she scrambles for purchase while I lick her up and down and back up again.

I pull back long enough to say, "You taste so good, Clio." Like citrus. It would be impossible to grow tired of the taste of her.

I bring my mouth to her clit and circle it with my tongue while my fingers make their way to her entrance. I stretch her rim slowly, teasingly, pairing the movements with the rhythm of my mouth. Her hips grind down onto my face and she is everything I taste, everything I smell, and everything I see as I keep my gaze on her, on the eyes I can just barely see above the fabric of her skirts. And those eyes are on me, too, though she looks like she's desperately fighting to keep them open.

I push a finger in and she tilts her head back far enough for me to see the *O* shape her mouth has fallen into, the pure bliss in the expression as I crook that finger against the pad inside of her, applying as I slide the finger back out. I do this a few more times until her hips start moving again, my silent sign that she's ready for more, and then I slip a second finger in and circle them around her, pressing against that pad before scissoring them inside her as I nip her clit with my teeth.

Her walls clench around my fingers and she lets out a sound that's half breathy moan and half sob as she comes, those muscles tightening and releasing, her hips bucking wildly. I pump my fingers inside of her as I work her through it, listening to her noises and ignoring how painfully hard my cock is in my pants as I climb over her and slide her dress the rest of the way off, until I'm left staring down at her naked body.

I press a kiss to her lips and notch a knee between her legs, something that'll help show me when she's come back up from the fall of her high. I bring one hand to each of her breasts as I kiss her and brush my thumbs against her nipples, teasing them into hard peaks before applying more pressure. Fuck, the feel of her... the sounds she makes... I never want to forget them. I never want to stop hearing them.

Clio begins to slide her core against my knee as I work her back into a heavy arousal, and her breath comes more quickly. I swear I can feel her body heating beneath mine.

Her delicate hands reach down to feel me, and she begins unbuckling my belt, opening her legs wide again, baring herself to me as she pulls my pants down just far enough for my length to spring free.

Clio sucks in a breath, her eyes on my cock. "Arthur, I..." she doesn't finish her sentence as she brings a hand to me, encircles me with those fingers. I reflexively roll my hips as I shudder at the feeling of her touching me. "You're..."

I don't make her finish her sentence. "You set the pace. Okay?"

She shudders, nods. "Be good to me."

I press a kiss to her lips. "Always."

I'm careful as I gently push myself into her. Her fingers grip onto my shoulders as she holds tight, but since I've already loosened her up and she's already climaxed, she's not nearly as tense as she would have been had we started with this.

She grips me tightly, and I exhale sharply as I sink in deep. I want to pound into her with everything I've got, but I refuse to break my promise to her, and so I let Clio show me when she's ready. I let her body set the pace, let her hips move before mine. I bring a hand down to her clit and tease it between my fingers, and Clio gasps and grinds her hips against me. "More," she breathes.

I give her more.

I go a little harder, a little faster, roll my hips a little differently. She meets me thrust for thrust, her mouth falling open and little sounds of arousal leaving her lips with each pump as our bodies meet.

"More," Clio says again as her head falls back, and we're both rolling our hips now, both trying to meet each other faster and faster. Release gathers at my spine, and from the fluidity of her movements, the way her body slides against mine and her walls clench me, I know she's getting close to her climax, too.

Her soft moans fill the surrounding air, and I cover her mouth to save us from being heard as they get louder and louder. She playfully licks my hand and sucks on a finger, and I wonder if she can taste herself on me from earlier.

Suddenly, she shifts and turns us both over to position herself on top, and she begins riding me.

"Fuck, Clio," I groan. I've had plenty of women on top before, but none have looked as good as her. I bring my free hand to one of her breasts and palm it, and she moves faster, harder. I give her a few uncontrolled movements before I can't hold on anymore, can't stop myself from gripping her hips to pump into her. I worry I'm going too hard, but she bucks and grinds her hips with surprising vigor. She throws her head back, her brilliant red hair flaring in an arc.

I sense the power coursing through her. She is like a goddess over me, completely in control of the situation. I had no idea she was so sensual and spirited.

Her breathing increases as she builds to a climax, her hips gyrating harder and harder. Her nails dig into my chest.

Clio screams as she climaxes, and a forceful gust of wind spreads out. Bushes are flattened and trees bend. The shockwave dissipates, leaving us both in shock.

Well, *that* certainly hadn't happened last time.

She stares down at me, her hair half covering her sweaty face. There's no denying that a powerful energy was just released from her. I felt the intensity of her power, yet I do not know what it may bring.

Chapter Twenty-Four

CLIO

Arthur and I talked long into the night, with me telling him exactly what that old man, Ecosar, had said to me.

We'd concluded that there must be some kind of magic within me, and if that were the case, then that would make me the first magic-user in decades. What that all means, exactly, is still unclear. Arthur had taken it all surprisingly well, although I could feel there was a lot he was keeping from me.

We slept in separate rooms last night, and I think we were both a little relieved about that. I don't think either of us wants to rush into anything. I still can't believe we'd done what we did.

I notice one thing, however, in the morning when Arthur and I meet in the gardens outside the tower. He is somewhat guarded today, and a little distant. He is still kind and considerate towards me, but I can tell a barrier has formed around him. I wonder if that barrier has always been there, protecting him from everyone.

We go through the breathing exercises Ecosar has given me. I have to perform a series of slow, deliberate movements, twisting my body and stretching my arms in a controlled manner, while focusing on my breaths. The breathing is the most important part. That, and clearing your mind to allow your inner self to come to the forefront. Whatever that means.

Arthur goes through the movements with me. He'd arrived sweaty after having gone for a run early in the morning, and at this point he is training with me shirtless. I try not to stare at his bulging, rippling muscles gleaming with perspiration in the sunlight. I've never seen anyone so toned and muscular before, like he has been carved from stone. I have to look away if I want to have a chance of keeping my hands off him and focus on my exercises.

We breathe and move together, arcing our arms and shifting our weight, with wide stances. Sometimes it feels like I'm meant to be pushing or pulling the air. With the sun beating down on us from over the tip of the tower, it's hot enough that I'm only wearing shorts that are overly large for me, and a sleeveless top.

I notice him glancing at me at times, but I also see how he's trying not to look at me. He's been looking at me differently, it feels. Like he's looking at someone else, or trying to see someone else on my face. It's hard to figure out. Or it could all just be in my head.

And I can't help but feel like he's pushing away from me. Maybe he's regretting what happened between us. Maybe he had just wanted to use me for my body. But if that were the case, he wouldn't be spending this time with me and wouldn't still be so nice to me.

I don't even know what I'm doing anymore. How could I be with an Oathlander? But, I don't see him as an Oathlander. Not in the way I used to think of these people. I only see the good man with a good heart, who sometimes seems to adore me.

I just wish I could understand what he's thinking.

When I try to clear my thoughts, I find a kind of peace washes over me while I breathe and move. The thrumming of energy courses through me for a second, before a burst of white light explodes from the tips of my fingers. It's like a bloom of white flame, and gone in an instant as though it never happened.

I almost fall and Arthur supports me with a hand on my lower back. We stare at each other for a moment, and I can feel the pull between us. His great chest is softly heaving. I have the urge the run my hands over his beard for some reason, and pull him to me. But I resist.

"Lady Fae," Arthur says with a grin.

I smile despite the troubling nerves causing my stomach to clench.

Then it's as if he remembers who we are and he pulls away with that guarded air, which deflates my shoulders. While he dabs at his face and torso with a towel, he says, "I have a book about magic and the Fae in my library. We can take a look if you like."

He's turned his back to me, like he's purposely trying to keep the distance between us. I hate how that bothers me so much.

I'm about to agree with his suggestion when I sense someone approaching.

A tall, muscular man in a crisp military uniform is stepping out of the tower, coming towards us. His dark hair curls down to his shoulders and he has similar sharply pointed brows to Arthur, though less pronounced. There is a cautious air about him, yet his demeanor comes across as aggressive. It's the first time I've felt like I'm in the presence of an enemy in the Oathlands, since getting to know Arthur better.

"Sorry to interrupt," the newcomer says, though I feel he's anything but sorry. "Arthur, may I have a word?"

"Of course," Arthur says, patting the towel on his arms. "Rourk. This is Clio. Clio, this is my brother, Rourk."

I nod politely and try to smile, though can't get the smile out. Arthur's brother returns my nod, going low enough for it to almost be a bow, though his dark eyes are watching me like a caged animal just waiting to be freed.

"Clio," Arthur says. "Why don't you go on ahead to the library and I'll catch up to you when I can?"

I nod again, feeling more comfortable addressing Arthur than his brother. My upbringing urges me to tell Rourk it was nice to meet him, and I tell him so, although it's simply politeness.

"Yes," he mutters as I walk away. "A pleasure to meet you, too..."

His words trail off, as though he meant to say something else. Like... my lady? His keen eyes are stuck on me as I leave, and even when I'm inside the tower, I feel them burning a hole in the back of my head.

Chapter Twenty-Five

CLIO

Well, that was an odd moment, I think as I make my way up the winding staircase to the library. Arthur must have told his brother about me. But I can't see what would warrant such animosity from him. It's not like he knows my true identity. Not even Arthur knows that.

I enter the library and feel calmer in the quiet space. I've always felt peaceful being surrounded by books when no one else is around.

Something shifts to my side and I notice I'm not alone. That young girl, May, is sitting between two tall bookshelves, her back against one of them. An enormous book is in her lap.

"Oh, I'm sorry," I say instinctively. "Would you prefer to be alone?"

"Yes. But, please stay. This library is big enough for the both of us." May gives me a warm smile. Her bright blue eyes contrast her long dark hair and her somewhat tanned complexion. I can see the resemblance between her and her father.

"That's very kind of you," I say.

May closes the book and regards me for a moment. "I have to ask. What's it like? Living in the Kingdom of Aer?"

My heart sinks, and a great wave of nausea pummels through me. I feel like I've had the ground swept from under me.

"E—excuse me?" I manage to say.

May stands and holds a calming hand out. "Oh, it's okay. I didn't mean to startle you. I guess... well, I know it's meant to be a secret and all. I was just wondering."

"I'm afraid you're mistaken," I tell her, and then I realize I don't actually have a story to tell her. I've thought at times what I would tell people if they asked me who I was or where I was from, but haven't actually come up with anything yet.

May smiles wanly. "You can't hide the truth, I'm afraid."

I steady myself with a hand on a shelf.

"Hey, come here. There's water. You look like you need to sit down."

She leads me to the tables at the center of the library. The air is now too thick and stuffy for me, but I try to breathe and calm myself. May pours me a glass of water from a pitcher.

"I won't tell anyone. I promise," she says.

"How... who else knows?"

She crunches her face. "I only told my father. He said he wasn't going to say anything. So, it's okay. We were just surprised you were the niece of King De'Kalo. That's very interesting, you know."

"How... *how* do you know?" I feel like the room is spinning a little.

"Ah, well, I... I have my ways," May says with a crooked grin, looking embarrassed. I don't know what to make of that, but I'm too fearful to ask.

She asks me about the Kingdom, and I decide to tell her some things. About how the city is much larger and much, much busier than the Oathlands. She'd be amazed at how many people there were. And some buildings are so tall they look like they'd pierce the sky.

I don't tell her how I think the Kingdom is much cleaner and more polished, with finer clothes and a better class of people. No, not better. Just a... a higher class of people. A difference in their way of life. Not to say one is better than the other.

"I know you guys are the enemy and everything," May says, "but I've always been fascinated by the Kingdom's rich history. More is known about the origins of the Kingdom than that of the Oathlands, before Queen Morgane founded the land."

"It's not such an easy way of life over there. Especially for someone like me." It's refreshing to be able to speak openly about myself. I want to trust this young girl, but the truth is that even if she has told half the people in the Oathlands, there's nothing I can do about that now. I have nothing left to hide.

"Someone like you?" she asks.

"I've always had to do what my father wanted of me. To do the right thing for my kingdom."

"Yeah. My father is the same," she says with a pouty frown. "He's always tried to tell me what to do. That's why

I'm living here in the tower. My father has often told me I could one day lead our people if I wanted, even if I'm not in line to the throne. I should learn to be a leader and a lady that everyone looks up to. But, I've never been interested in any of that. I just want to be a historian. I've always been more comfortable with books than with people."

I find myself smiling at her. "You know, you and your uncle have a way of being honest and open so quickly. I'm in awe of that."

May shrugs dismissively. "Uncle Arthur has always told me I should be whoever I am, and not apologize for it or try to hide it."

"He is a wise man. And, I can relate. I also feel more comfortable in my own company than with others."

I can't stop thinking about Arthur potentially knowing my true identity. His brother must have told him by now. Maybe that's what they're talking about right now. A part of me expects Arthur to burst through the door at any moment and throw me into a cell for lying to him.

May notices my empty glass and pours me some more water.

I thank her and mention the book I came looking for. About magic and Fae. "And... is there a book about this Queen Morgane? I've heard her name a few times now and would be interested in learning more about her."

May's bright eyes flash with eagerness. She hops up and shows me around the bookshelves, pointing out the various sections and explaining the filing system. She seems to know everything about the library and practically knows where to find every book, despite there being thousands of books.

We collect a few books and settle down at the tables. I spend some time looking through the books, losing track of time. Mostly, I try not to think about Arthur and absorb myself in the books. It's nice not to have to talk to anyone or be a certain way around people.

May calls over a guard who has been standing by the door, and requests a cheese board platter.

"There's something about having cheese and crackers when I'm studying," she tells me after the guard leaves.

We discuss what we like to include in our cheese boards, such as cured meats and grapes, and for a while I feel comfortable with her, getting to know her quirks and character. We both agree that soft cheeses are better than hard cheeses for crackers.

"Oh, and you have to have some fruit dips on the board," May exclaims.

I raise my brows. "What's a fruit dip? We don't have those."

"Really? Wow! You're going to love them. Just wait and see. Red mango is my favorite."

We settle back to reading for a while.

I read a chapter in a history book that disturbs me. The First King of the Kingdom, Valron De'Kalo, was once married to the First Queen of the Oathlands, Morgane the Mother. They had cast Morgane out of the Kingdom after many arguments and building resentment with her husband. She had wandered the land for days with a small contingent of her loyal followers.

Years later, after she had set up her new home in the Red Marshes, which would later be known as the Oathlands, King De'Kalo sent men to murder the Queen. According to this book, that began the centuries-long war between the two kingdoms. Apparently, the king had sought to murder his wife while they'd been together, after he'd learned she was planning to take over the kingdom for herself. They had been trying to kill each other for years. So it's hard to say who was at fault and who really started the first war. But it's clear that the murder of the Queen at the hands of the Kingdom triggered the animosity between the kingdoms. An animosity that would endure throughout the years, causing countless deaths and wars, not to mention endless skirmishes.

I'm amazed at what I'm reading, because none of this is in our Kingdom's historical records. I ask May a few questions and she clarifies what I'm reading as though it's basic knowledge.

I read about how the Kingdom was to blame for the murder of several members of the Oathlands royal families, including their children. I know both sides have killed many people, but I hadn't realized just how fiendish and devious the Kingdom has been throughout the years.

The more I read, the more I understand that the Kingdom has hidden things and changed history to make themselves appear in the right, and make the Oathlands out to be the enemy. So much so that other lands fell to the side of the Kingdom and took the truth that word of the Oathlands as lies.

"How can I trust words on a page?" I ask her, feeling nauseous.

"How can you trust the words of people? Books do not need to lie, especially ones as old as this." May shrugs, then adds, "People tend to fabricate stories as generations pass, as they go from mouth to ear to mouth to ear. They want to think of new ways to tell it, better ways to say things. Sometimes they tell white lies to make the story more interesting, thinking it's harmless. But those white lies can grow until they change the truth, make it something it isn't. And sometimes those white lies don't start so small. Sometimes they start bigger." May shrugs. "But the point is, you can't trust people anymore than you can trust that book." She gestures to the book in front of me. "That is the truth. You can choose to accept it or not."

"But you understand how difficult this is? To accept this truth that goes against everything I've ever believed? Just because someone wrote the words down? Who's to say these aren't lies and our books in the Kingdom tell the truth?"

There's a burning sensation in my skirt pocket. The crystal is thrumming quietly and has started to burn. I tentatively bring it out and see it is cool to the touch.

May is instantly intrigued by the crystal, and I tell her what it is.

"Oh, wow. Is that a real Fae crystal? I've only seen pictures of them before. I had a necklace with a pretend Fae crystal when I was younger. I used to tell people I was Fae, and would fake wings."

"I think it's real," I tell her.

Her brows shoot up. "I have an idea. Okay, so... well... you see, I have a sort of... ability. It tells me what people are thinking or feeling. I get it sometimes when I touch people."

"You are magical?" I ask in awe.

"No, no. It's not magic. I... well, no one knows what it is. It's just a feeling I get sometimes. I think I've had it all my life. It doesn't always work and I haven't figured out how to control it exactly. Only my father and uncle know about it. I've... tried to pretend I don't have it in me, and I guess it's why I prefer to keep my own company. I can't get into any trouble touching books."

"That must be a difficult gift to have."

"Well, it's... it is what it is. So anyway, I was thinking... I could touch your hand, and see if I can sense anything hiding inside your mind. It has to be skin to skin."

Skin to skin makes me think of being with Arthur. I shake my head. "I'm not sure about that."

May insists and tells me I won't come to any harm. She swears to keep what she sees between us. I can't fully trust her, but in the end, I agree to try it. I'm actually intrigued to see this ability of hers. She knows my true identity, so there must be some truth in what she's saying, and I had felt nothing back when we'd shaken hands.

I put my hand on the table, and May gently presses her hand over mine.

Nothing happens. Then, after a few seconds, I'm bombarded with sounds, smells, and images, like I'm seeing through other people's eyes. I can even taste many different things. Everything hits me at once, but I somehow understand it all.

In an instant, I know the truth. The truth of who I am.

I see a great war, and the Oathlands is on fire. My father is there on the battlefield, much younger, in bloodied armor, cutting down Oathlands soldiers and civilians. I watch through his eyes as he finds a baby in the crib. He takes that baby back to the kingdom and presents it to his wife. They raise the girl as their own.

The bombardment of my senses cuts off when May removes her hand. I drop to the table with my hands spread, my breath sharp and shallow. The crystal is bright and hot as it clatters and rolls free from my grip, its light diminishing. There is a light sheen of sweat on May's pale face.

I understand now. I was... born in the Oathlands. Taken as a baby and raised in the Kingdom. Kidnapped from my true family.

I think I'm going to vomit.

It's clear from May's shimmering wide eyes that she had seen what I'd seen. The crystal lays dormant beside my hand.

"You're... an Oathlander?" May says in an awed whisper. "You're...?" She gets up. "I have to tell my uncle."

"May, no wait. Stop!" I get up, but she is already at the door.

"I'm sorry, he has to know!" she yells as she bursts out, leaving me alone in the library.

I'm shaken as I sit there in the silence. Had the crystal somehow interfered with May's ability? Shown us things we weren't meant to know? How had all of that been inside my head? The crystal must have shown us more than what's in my mind.

So I'm... an Oathlander? Can that really be true?

I startle when I notice I'm not alone. Someone is walking up to me. Then I relax when I see it's just one of Arthur's guards.

I'm familiar with him, as he's been particularly nice and accommodating to me.

"Felix," I say. "You startled me. Is everything alright?"

It's rare for one of the guards to get this close to me. He comes to a stop with a smile, his hands clasped behind him.

"Everything is just fine, my lady. At least, everything will be. Once I deal with you."

He raises the long dagger he had hidden behind his back.

"I'm afraid your stay in the Oathlands has come to an end."

Chapter Twenty-Six

CLIO

I try to move but I'm frozen with fear. "Felix, what are you..."

The guard grins at me, but there is no hint of the friendly man I've known in his malicious eyes.

He rears the knife up and plunges it down. I scream and throw myself back, leaving the knife to swing through the air. My chair topples back and I tumble to the ground, my skirt flaring around me as I roll to get away from him.

Felix is surprisingly fast as he rushes around the table, the dagger up, ready to kill. I push myself to my feet and grab a chair to throw it in his path. The chair catches Felix's feet and sends him crashing to the ground.

I consider grabbing the dagger but it is still firmly in his hand, and I want to get as far away from him as I can.

He's blocking my route to the door so I run into the lanes of bookshelves to go through the outer path to the door. I hear him getting up and continuing his pursuit of me, but I can't see him among the shelves of books surrounding me.

For a long moment, there is nothing but silence in the room as I pause and catch my breath, pressed against a shelf. I hardly dare to breathe. I have a feeling that if I run out from the cover of the shelves, he will pounce on me. My heart is throbbing violently in my chest.

"You should never have come here, my lady," Felix says, his location hard to pinpoint. "But you couldn't have known that I was like you. They say that Kingdom folk recognize their own, and Oathlanders recognize the stench of their own. But you couldn't see who I really was. Your father was very surprised to get the message I sent him. He knows you're here, princess, and he is coming for you, with all the might of the Kingdom. Our Kingdom."

I take a second to realize what he's saying.

"Yes, princess. I am from the Kingdom, like you." His voice is growing louder and clearer, telling me he's closing in on me. "Eleven years I've been here, posing as one of them, feeding information back to my people. They would hold me a hero for helping return the princess to the Kingdom. But that is not what I want. I'm sick of these filthy Oathlanders, and I want them wiped out once and for all. Once I learned the Kingdom military was coming for you, I knew there was only one thing to do. There's nothing like fueling a great war than the death of a royal family member."

He doesn't just want to kill me. Felix plans to make me a martyr.

Silence comes over us again. Until Felix leaps into view at the end of the bookshelves. I scream and run towards the door, but when I leave the shelving units and rush out into the open, Felix charges toward me. He tackles me to the ground and we tumble as I scramble to break free, but he is so strong.

"Get away!" I yell.

I try to summon the magic within me, but I'm too distracted and shaken. I hardly know how I had summoned it in the first place, back when I'd scared off that monster. And it had taken a lot of focus just to summon a spark from my fingers during my training earlier.

Felix climbs on top of me, pinning me down. He grabs my head and slams it on the ground. My vision swims and blurs as pain ignites in my skull.

He rises and crouches over me, raising the knife high. "I'm sorry, princess. But your death is needed to start the next war."

I've been reaching desperately to the side and have managed to grab a fallen book. When the knife slices down towards me, I bring the book to my chest and the blade stabs into it, the tip barely missing my skin.

I twist the book, causing him to lose his grip on the knife, and throw the book away with the knife embedded in it.

Felix spits out a curse, murder flashing in his eyes. "I'll just have to kill you with my bare hands."

I scream for him to stop as he reaches down for me.

A great hulking beast crashes into Felix, throwing him to the ground. Felix and the large creature roll and wrestle, until I realize they aren't wrestling. The great hairy beast is tearing into Felix, its claws tearing chunks of his flesh. Blood and clothing fly out from the mangled corpse.

I'm frozen in shock and fear, not daring to move. The hairy beast finally stops tearing Felix apart, and it stands there on its hind legs, its back to me, panting heavily.

It's the same creature who had attacked me the other night. Now it must be back to kill me. To kill everyone it can find.

The beast turns to me suddenly, and I yelp at the sight of its glowing red eyes. It snarls, but it seems to calm down a little.

Then, before my eyes, I watch as it begins to... shrink. Its fur retracts inwards and its muscles diminish, turning into the shape of a man. A naked man. Within seconds, the beast is no longer there and I'm left looking at a large, muscular man.

"Arthur?" I say in shock.

It really is him. He's standing there now, completely nude.

He takes a step closer, but I push myself back along the floor.

"It's okay. You're safe," he says. I still can't believe it's really him.

I can't help but let my eyes roam, taking in his body and seeing whether he's hurt. At least until I get distracted. Noting where my eyes land, he picks up a book and places it in front of his groin.

"Ah... I suppose I have some explaining to do," he says.

I slowly rise onto shaky legs. "You. You were that... that thing? The whole time? How? Why?"

"That is a long story. Let's go and talk about it, shall we?"

I glance at the bloodied, torn remains of Felix and almost gag.

Arthur comes closer and his presence is a soothing comfort. "May babbled some things to me. She sounded insane."

"I think we both have some explaining to do," I agree.

I'm keenly aware of him being naked, and a book being the only thing between us.

"I think you're going to have to find a larger book to hide your modesty," I say, which makes him chuckle.

He drops the book and grins at me, his desire burning clearly in his eyes. I feel the overwhelming urge to leap on him, but before I have a chance to move, we both become aware of someone entering the library.

May pauses at the door and, at the sight of her naked uncle, screams and runs.

Chapter Twenty-Seven

CLIO

A few hours later, Arthur and I are up on the roof of his tower, talking and sipping wine with a plate of cheese and bread between us.

After everything that's happened, I find my chaotic mind drifting to the fruit dips May had mentioned. The ones I never got to try. I wonder if I'll ever get to try them. I'm still shaken from almost having been killed. I've never been so afraid before in my life. But I'm glad, now more than ever, to have Arthur beside me.

Once my mind had cleared enough to form cohesive thoughts, the first thing I'd told Arthur was what Felix had said to me. About having sent a message to the Kingdom. About my father coming to the Oathlands with the full force of the Kingdom military.

Arthur had gone straight to his brother to give the warning. Felix may have been bluffing, but we can't take that chance. The Oathlands soldiers will be searching the nearby land to see if an army is approaching.

Arthur has assured me we have nothing to worry about, and that he doesn't believe there is an army coming for us. For now, he's been focused on me, and making sure I'm alright. He's told me to put my faith in their soldiers, and that's what I have to do.

I'm just afraid that a warning horn will blow at any second.

I've told Arthur about my vision with May. How I now know that I was born in the Oathlands and taken away shortly after my birth. There is no doubt in my mind that what I had seen was the truth. I can feel it in my bones. And I'm furious with my father for keeping that from me.

My entire life has been a lie.

We look out at the glorious views, which I'm still in awe of, as the sun slowly sets. The sky is clear this evening and there are few clouds around to hide from the sun, which makes me feel even more like I'm out hovering in the open sky. Like I'm on the top of the world.

I eye the distant mountains, knowing the Kingdom is somewhere beyond them. And I shudder. I really don't know what to think about that place anymore.

I listen intently as Arthur tells me how he can change into that beast.

"My mother was a good woman," he begins. "But in her attempt to make the world a better place, she drew the wrath of a witch with evil in her heart. The witch cursed my mother, who was at the time pregnant with me. She told my mother that she would birth a monster. I arrived seemingly okay, but it wasn't until my eighth birthday that I first changed. I've grown up alongside the beast within me ever since. At first, the monster completely took over, and I would wake up with a hole in my memory. As time went on, I learned to gain some control of my actions and have some sense of myself inside the beast. Now, I can fully control the transformation and can control my actions as the beast."

"You could not control the transformations before?"

He looks out at the fiery horizon as he says, "At first, I would transform during times of great anger. Or even happiness. For a time, any great emotional shift would cause a transformation. That was something else I eventually conquered."

"That must have been a difficult time for you, growing up. It's not always easy to control our emotions."

"I've learned to dampen them, and shut them down when I have to."

"That explains why you're so good at brooding."

He almost smiles at that, but a heavy expression weighs him down. He looks so troubled.

"Arthur," I say, voicing a burning question. "Why did you attack me as the beast?"

He makes a sour face, looking guilty. "I had wanted to see what magic you had in you. At the time, I thought you were hiding your magical gifts from me, and I figured you would bring them out if you thought your life was in danger. I hadn't known you were only just learning about your magical lineage. I apologize for attacking you, but I assure you I would never have hurt you."

"I trust you," I say, and the words surprise me. I really do trust him. "But what if I'd killed you?"

He shrugs. "Then I would have gotten my answer about your magic, yes?"

I blink at him, then shake my head. "You're mad, you know that?"

What a foolish thing to do. I could have, if I'd known more of my magic. I could have really hurt him—or, at least, the beast he'd shifted into. Such a unique creature. "I've... seen nothing like it before."

"It is a monster with no name. Born into this world just for me."

My mind struggles to comprehend everything I'm hearing. I've reached the point where I mostly feel numb. "I'm surprised a witch could curse your mother like that. I didn't think anyone had such a power."

"We say there is no magic left in the world, but that is not entirely true. There are ghostly remnants, or shadows, of power scattered around. But for the most part, there is practically no magic left."

"Until now," I mutter.

"Until now," he agrees. "Now that you have begun to explore your Fae heritage."

I shake my head. "Well, at least now we have it all out in the open."

I still can't believe I have Fae blood in me. But I feel free to talk about everything now that we both know all there is to know about each other. Arthur had confessed to me that his brother Rourk had told him I was the niece of King De'Kalo, and that has made me feel freer to be myself with him.

"Actually," he says, turning to me. "There is something I have to tell you. Something I discovered... about you."

I grimace, not wanting to hear any more revelations.

"It's not that bad," he quickly says. "Actually, it's something good. That birthmark on your shoulder. It's the mark of the—"

"The Oathlands royal family," I cut in. "I... I know. That was one thing I'd felt in the vision. There had been so much going on, but now you said it, and I said it out loud, I know it's the truth."

My mind spins with unsettled thoughts that have the potential to consume and overwhelm me.

"What does this mean?" I ask after a silence.

"Did you discover who your parents are inside that vision?"

I shake my head. "They must have been a part of the old royal family."

"Those birthmarks have always been something of a mystery. But you must carry some of the royal line blood in you for it to appear."

"There must be some mistake." After everything that's happened, I don't think I have the brain capacity to handle this. "Does... this make us related?"

He chuckles softly. "The royal line ended so long enough ago that it has been spread and diluted over the generations by many people. This doesn't make us related. Not by blood, anyway. I didn't even think there was such a thing as a royal line anymore. But I suppose I was naïve to think that."

I sip my wine while I try to take everything in. It's a wonder how different I feel now, after a handful of days in the Oathlands. It feels like I've been here for months. I've not only discovered that I'm descended from a magical race of people, but I'm somehow next in line to the throne of the Oathlands. Not to mention that my father was actually my kidnapper.

Despite not being hungry, I reach for a piece of bread to have something to do. Arthur is also reaching out and our hands meet. We stare at each other for a moment, before he pulls his hand away. I turn from him, burning from the rush of rejection..

But I turn back to him and say, "I want you to know that if you have changed your mind about... well... if you feel differently, or if you've decided you don't feel anything towards me. I will understand. I know we haven't really said anything about what's going on, but..."

"You are a remarkable person, Clio De'Kalo. Do you know that?" Arthur cuts off my babble and there is awe in his voice. "I've been expecting that you would see me differently, now that you know of the beast within me."

He looks out to the horizon. "My whole life, I've felt like I wasn't worthy of love. I've actually... I've never been loved by anyone before. I've been with women, but none have loved me. Not truly loved me. They might have convinced themselves for a time, and some may have only liked me for my looks, or my position, or because they thought I was someone else. Someone they had made up in their heads. But the truth is, no one has ever truly loved all of me."

He slowly turns to me, his eyes glistening in the golden light. "If you want to leave, you are free to do so. I will no longer hold you here. I think I've been keeping you here for the wrong reasons."

I give that some thought. "You know, I don't feel like I have a home to go back to anymore. I was born in the

Oathlands, and, while the Kingdom of Aer has been the only home I've ever known, I can't bring myself to go back there. Not just yet, anyway."

"You are welcome to stay here until you figure things out."

His deep, dark eyes draw me in, and I can see the emotion shining in them.

"Here," he says, breaking the silence. "I have something to show you."

He gets up and helps me to stand, and we go over to look out at the back of the tower. He points to an open field beyond the grounds, before the ground rises and the cliffs begin. The ground has been dug up and cleared so that there are large square sections of dirt. I'm sure there were a few trees in that spot that are no longer there.

"What am I looking at?" I ask.

"That is your field. The one you said you wanted."

I look at him, confused.

"I'm readying the soil. I'm afraid I have nothing to plant yet as I have nothing to give you, but I'm working on that. Anyway, I wanted you to know that you had a place here, if you stayed. You can have your fields and have the laborers you need, just like you wanted. You can have anything you want, if you stay."

I'm blown away by the gesture. "Oh, Arthur," is all I can say as I'm left speechless. No one has ever done something like this for me.

When I look at him, I really see him looking back. Like he can see me more than anyone else ever has. Sees and accepts me for who I am. That's all I've ever wanted.

"Thank you for everything. I don't know what to say right now. I'll tell you when I know what I want to do." My mind is too muddled to think about any decisions.

I reach out and hold his hand. "I want you to know I care about you deeply."

He draws closer and we lean into each other. We kiss, as though it were the easiest, simplest thing in the world.

Our hands moved eagerly across each other's bodies, every touch sparking a fire that neither of us wanted to extinguish. Now we're started, there's no stopping us. I can't tear his clothes off fast enough. His shirt rips under my fingers and falls away, revealing the hard planes of muscles across his chest. My dress slides down easily from around my hips, falling to the roof below us. We strip and use our clothes to lay on, settling ourselves on top of the fabric before our mouths meet again.

He doesn't bother with his fingers or his mouth this time, and though he *was* quite skilled at that, I find I'm much too impatient for all of him to want any of that tonight, anyway. I look up to see the first stars coming out in the darkening sky, washed with red.

I lift my hips and wrap my legs around his waist, rolling myself against his length as he kisses me, working us both up. I feel myself growing wetter and wetter, and his length hardens with each brush of my body against his. His hands mold to my breasts and I moan as he palms them, pinching and rolling the nipples. It's a very low sort of pleasure, mixed with pain. It'll leave my breasts sore, but it's worth it.

Arthur waits until I'm already gasping before sinking himself inside of me in one push. I cry out as my body stretches to accommodate him quickly.

I'll be sore *there* tomorrow, too.

Again—couldn't care less.

Especially as I press myself so tightly against him I feel his body against my clit. It spurs me onward, and I bounce myself against him, wanting more, demanding it. He is more than willing to give it to me. Arthur becomes more forceful this time, less reserved and restrained, and I enjoy how he gets a little rough and wild with me. I hunger for him and can't get enough of the feel of him inside me.

I feel my release building at the base of my spine, but force myself to hold on, unwilling to be done with him, with this, with us right now.

Even as my inner walls clench him, he rubs deliciously against that spot inside of me and his fingers work my nipples. He brushes again and again against that spot inside of me. I don't want to let go, but I don't know how much longer I'll be able to hold on.

"Arthur," I whimper. "I'm going to come."

"Then come," he says, his voice rough. He punctuates that statement with a brush against my g-spot.

"I d-don't want to stop." My words come out hitched as I fight to hold myself back, though I can't help but work my hips against him even still.

"Then we won't." His words are simple, matter of fact. "Come, Clio. We'll keep going."

At his words, I lose it. I buck wildly on him as I orgasm, and Arthur grunts as he pounds us through it. And when I'm still, pulls out.

I protest. "But—"

He cuts me off with a chuckle. "Patience, Clio."

Before I can get another word in, he turns me to face away from him and wraps an arm around my waist, sliding me against him so that I'm on my knees. He spreads my legs further apart and, without warning, sinks right back into me.

My body responds instantly, pleased at the feeling of him inside of me. His fingers work my clit now, bringing me back up to the same high as him quickly, until our bodies are pushing and pulling together once more.

He pulls out and slams back in twice as hard. I scream with the ecstasy of it, rolling my hips back against him, and his other hand grips my ass, squeezing it in his hand as he thrusts himself in and out of me. This new angle stimulates me in an entirely different way, but still hits the deepest part of me as he sinks in and out and in and out.

My walls constrict as I fight the urge to come yet again, but Arthur says, "*I* can't hold on anymore, Clio. Please. Come with me."

I nod, and with one last thrust, we're both letting ourselves loose, our orgasms shattering us together. He pumps through it, and I back myself against him, milking the last of the pleasure from our bodies until we're both still, and he pulls me against him.

We lay there for some time, holding each other. The sky is much darker the next time I notice it. We simply stare at each other while he idly plays with a strand of my hair, and I run my fingers over his chest. Right now, I only want to be here in Arthur's arms, breathing in his intoxicating, warm musk.

"You don't have to worry about how I feel about you," I whisper to him. I feel the urge to tell him more. To find the words to express how deeply my heart sings for him at this moment.

But something detonates below us, rocking the tower. A great plume of fire explodes across the town, lighting the night sky. Fiery arrows rain down into the town, looking like tiny firebugs from this distance.

The Oathlands is under attack. The Kingdom is here.

Chapter Twenty-Eight

CLIO

My heart is pounding as I rush down the stairwell of the tower, hearing the booming sounds of battle echoing outside. Arthur and I quickly dressed, and he told me to stay hidden inside. Then he had leapt off the tower again. But this time he hadn't just dropped down like before. He had jumped and soared a long distance, easily clearing his garden borders. I've never seen such a feat like it.

Two tower guards find me in the hallway as I leave the stairwell.

"Come, ma'am, we will escort you to your room," one of them says.

I tell them I have to do one thing first, and they follow me down the hall to the winding staircase at the end. We go down two levels and I come to the library door. I open the door and call out for May, but there is no answer. I can't see from here if Felix's maimed body is still there, or if they have cleared away him by now. And I don't want to know.

When I go back into the hallway, I hear rushing footsteps. May is running towards me, her eyes wide with terror.

"Clio, what's going on?" she says, gripping my shoulders with shaky hands.

"The town is under attack and we must get to safety," I tell her. She wants me to go to her room, where we can see out into the town. We're accompanied by three guards now as we make our way up to May's sleeping quarters. I recognize one guard as the gruff older man with the graying hair, Cheston, who seems to be the most experienced and clear-headed of all the guards I've met so far.

We reach May's room and Cheston follows us inside while the two other guards remain outside the door. The main room is long and looks to be for lounging and hosting, while sliding doors to the side must lead to her bedroom. The scent of perfumed roses is strong in the air. May and I rush to the window on the far end and look out.

Several fires rage throughout the town, and the sounds of screaming and yelling carry in the wind, along with the clashing of swords. I press a hand to my mouth, horrified at what I'm seeing.

Why is the Kingdom attacking so brutally? This is not the rescue attempt I had been hoping for over the past few days. Unless they're not here just to save me. They must want to send a message to the Oathlanders to never even consider kidnapping any of their people again. They don't want to just punish the Oathlanders; they want to make them suffer for years to come in the aftermath.

I'm not one of your people, I think, gritting my teeth. They took me. *Stole* me. Taught me to hate my own people.

"They're going to kill everyone," May says, on the edge of tears, shaking beside me.

Cheston is standing nearby, frowning. "They want to cause destruction more than death. They mean to destroy what they can. Any casualties will be inconsequential to them."

Everyone knows the Kingdom military outnumbers the Oathlands military three-to-one these days. They could very well overpower the town if the full military is here.

Out in the darkness, highlighted against the deep amber of flames rising into the misty air, I think I see Arthur bounding over rooftops.

I notice Cheston's severe grimace as he looks out at the chaos.

"You want to be out there, fighting?" I say.

He remains still, like a statue. "My task is to keep you both safe."

"And what if I gave you new orders?" I ask.

"You do not have the authority to supersede Lord Bearon's orders, ma'am."

"Well, what about me?" May says indignantly. "I am a Bearon. If you wish, you can do what you like to protect us. If that means you desire to go out there and fight."

The gruff Cheston almost cracks a sad smile. "You cannot give me orders either, in this instance, young ma'am."

We watch as the war rages on. There is no doubt about what we're seeing. A war. Like the Last Blood War. Except this feels more like an invasion.

Pillars of smoke are rising into the starry night sky, the atmosphere bathed in a horrible fiery light. I feel so helpless just standing here, knowing I can't contribute to the fighting, or help put an end to it.

Below, we see dark figures rushing through the gardens. King's Guard, in their white polished armor. They must have broken through the gate. May yelps in fear at the sight of them.

Cheston curses. "Stay here," he says to us as he hurries out of the room to give orders to the guards.

May and I can hear fighting out in the gardens, but we can't see anything from our window. Then I notice a figure running frantically. I recognize him as the groundskeeper, Dio. Three men of the King's Guard have him cornered, and they're approaching with their swords out. Dio trips and is pleading for his life, crying and blubbering.

I've seen enough, and I've been helpless long enough.

I turn to May. "Stay in the room. I'll be right back after I help the groundskeeper."

She tries to go with me, but I firmly insist she stays. When we both open the door, we see one guard has remained in the hallway.

"You need to keep Lord Bearon's niece safe," I direct him as we step out.

The guard tries to stop us both, but only manages to hold May back.

"I'm sorry, May," I tell her as I back away. "I will be back. I promise."

I'm certain the King's Guard won't hurt me once they see who I am. I'm hoping they'll listen to their princess and let the groundskeeper go. Leave us alone in the tower. I can't just stand and watch as people suffer around me.

When I get to the main doors to the tower, I find them bolted shut, so I leave them alone and head out of a side door. The night is alive with thick smoke and the sounds of battle.

I run around the tower into the gardens to find the guards surrounding the groundskeeper, but I see the bloodied remains of Dio, and I scream in shock. I'm too late. The King's Guard turn to me and ready their swords.

The thrumming of energy courses through me as I glare at them, hating them.

"I am your princess and I order you to cease this madness!" I yell with clenched fists.

There's a moment of hesitation before realization comes over them.

"Princess. You must follow us. We will take you to safety," one guard says. There are so many in the King's Guard that I don't think I recognize any of these men.

"I'm not going anywhere," I say, stepping back. "I demand you stop this fighting at once."

"We cannot do that, my lady," the guard says.

I stand firm. "Then take me to my father."

He is the only one who can stop this. I know now that I must find my father and convince him to stop the attack.

The guards agree, and I leave with them. I look up to see May watching me out of the window, looking very sad and afraid. I hate to leave the girl, but I know she will be safe there.

I'm sorry, May. I will be back. I promise.

I hope I don't break my oath to her.

I hope, more than anything, that I get to see Arthur again.

Chapter Twenty-Nine

CLIO

I'm taken into town by the King's Guard, the booming echoes of battle ringing out all around. I pray for Arthur's safety within the chaos.

Several armed figures come out from around a corner and charge at us. The Oathlands military. I'm pushed back by a King's Guard as the two groups clash, swords flashing and battle staffs swinging. It's four King's Guard against five Oathlands soldiers, until several more Kingdom soldiers arrive. The soldiers in blue and silver armor join their brothers in the white of the King's Guard.

One King's Guard breaks free and comes to me, gripping me by the elbow.

"Come, my lady, we must continue on. Your father awaits."

I allow myself to be taken by him as the fight continues behind us. The sight of men being slain sends a violent shiver through me.

"Where is my father?"

The guard points ahead. "He is by the bridges, near a park on the upper level."

I know that to be the Lipadil Bridges, the three bridges that connect to the area with Groven Park.

People rush by us as we go, some crying and screaming for their lives. My heart aches for the terror these people are going through. I've never been in a war like this. Never knew it could be so brutal. People are being slain by Kingdom soldiers, and the fires rage on. This is madness.

In the distance, I think I hear the roar of what could be Arthur's beast form. I imagine him charging about and tearing into the Kingdom's soldiers, like I'd seen him do to Felix.

We enter a wide street that's been devastated. Many windows are blown out, carts and stalls are strewn about, and two fires burn in bordering streets, smoke and flames rising over the rooftops. I cough in the smothering air.

Cries off to the side get my attention. There is an older couple with two young girls hiding under a fallen market stall. They are crying and their wide eyes are pleading and full of fear. I break away from the guard and rush over to the family. The guard urges me to keep going, but I ignore him.

"It's okay. Come here. Come to me," I say, waving them to come out from their hiding place. The girls are crying and I wish I could just make them feel better.

I manage to coax the family out, after convincing them I mean to help them and that the King's Guard with me isn't going to hurt them. I see a row of houses are to the side, lead them to the nearest door, and bang on it.

"Please, we need help. Please help us," I call out as I bang on the door, and then rush over to the next door and bang on that.

The second door opens and we see an elderly woman. I don't have time to explain everything, but I manage to convince her to let the family come inside. Not that I need to do much convincing, as the old woman is eager to help. I see there are more people inside, and I wonder if she is also sheltering others from the chaos.

I head back into the street with the King's Guard, and it's not long before we come across another battle between Oathland and Kingdom soldiers. Flaming arrows fly overhead, cutting through the dark sky, their origins and destinations unknown. The guard leads me down a side alley, but I urge him to keep going to the next street, which will take us toward our destination.

My thoughts shift to Arthur. I know he can be headstrong and I dearly hope he won't be harmed tonight. I listen and look out for any signs of him while we run up some stairs carved into the hill, hoping to get a hint of his location.

The destruction all around devastates me. What had once been peaceful streets with warm, kind people, now look like the six hells have come down on them. We pass dead bodies strewn along the road. I wonder if I had met any of the fallen people before.

I tighten my fist and feel a growing power inside me. But I know I can't yet control nor command my magical ability yet. I can't even summon it at will. For all I know, I'm good just for a light show.

Two Oathlands soldiers run into us and immediately engage in battle with the King's Guard accompanying me, who push me away. I duck to the side of the street and merge into the shadows as they fight. The two soldiers quickly dispatch of the lone King's Guard, but I have no interest in any of them. I must find my father. As the brother of the King, he will be able to end this madness if he wants.

I consider picking up a fallen sword, but decide against it. I've had some formal training, but I will certainly be no match for an experienced soldier. It's best not to show myself as a fighter at all, since I'll have no chance against them. Not all Kingdom soldiers will recognize me as their princess before their swords meet my belly, so I can only run and hide and do my best.

An elderly man has fallen ahead, losing control of his walking stick. I detour to help him stand back up before making my way up the inclining street towards Groven Park. A great wall of fire blocks the route ahead, so I double back and duck into an alley to cut across. I hope I don't end up getting myself lost amid all this chaos. My memory of these streets is rudimentary at best. I pass a body on the ground that is on fire and wince. So much death.

At the end of this next street, I'll have a clearer view of the bridge that will take me across to where my father should be. I hope.

My path is blocked when Kingdom soldiers charge at me. A rush of bodies comes from behind and Oathlands soldiers run by me and intercept the attackers. I watch them battle and in less than a minute, only three Oathlands soldiers remain standing. It's then I see that one of my defenders is Rourk, Arthur's brother.

His armor is bloodied, and one of his pauldrons is missing. With a longbow strapped to his back and a sword in one hand and dagger in the other, he looks every bit the seasoned warrior.

"You should not be out here," he says stiffly, clearly not happy to see me.

"I need to get to the Lipadil Briges. I... my father is near there. I must see him and get him to stop this madness."

"You mean you want him to rescue you. Take you back home." Rourk's fierce eyes glower at me.

I return the expression. "I have no home in the Kingdom," I say sharply, which catches him off guard. "But if my father wants my return, if it will mean the end of the attack, I will go with him."

He sighs and shakes his head. "If you want me to argue with you, girl, to convince you to stay, then you've come to the wrong man. The sooner we are rid of you, the better."

"I don't want that," I answer through gritted teeth. "I just don't want these deaths on my hands."

Rourk stares at me for a long moment, and then simply nods and turns. He and the soldiers march off, clearly meaning for me to follow. There was something left unspoken between us. Does he want to help me for his brother's sake? Does he know the two of us have gotten close? I find Rourk as infuriatingly hard to read as Arthur.

I want to tell him that I truly do not want to leave the Oathlands, that I want to stay with his brother. But if I can stop this war by returning to the Kingdom with my father, then that is what I must do.

"Have you seen Arthur?" I ask as we climb up a set of stairs, reaching the highest area in town.

"Not for some time," Rourk says. "But if there is one man I worry least about, it's my brother."

I've seen Arthur fight, and seen what he can do in his beast form, but I still fear greatly for his safety.

We crest a hill and come to a flat field of grass, where we can see one of the Lipadil Bridges ahead. Across on the next platform, I think I see my father among a group of soldiers and King's Guard on the roof of a short building. Of course, my father would want a good view of the battlefield. I wonder if Leonas is with him, but I know my fiancé has no head for battle and wouldn't dare enter one, even if it meant trying to save his love.

Fires rage all around, and it's now I can see the full extent of the destruction to the Oathlands. I want to scream and cry, but I have to stay strong if I am going to confront my father.

No, stop calling him that. You know he is not your father. My chaotic mind spins, throbbing my temple.

The two soldiers with us begin to cross the bridge, and Rourk instructs me to go after them so he can take up the rear.

The wooden bridge is loose and rickety, the boards beneath my feet quite far apart and giving way too much for my liking. I hold on to the rope railing on the sides as I make my way, hoping I don't slip and fall off. There's about twenty feet to cross, and below there is only darkness in the deep fissure.

Streaks of light fly through the sky, coming for us. The flaming arrows rain down on us, many zipping by, some hitting a board or the rope railing. I scream as the bridge rocks violently. I try to support myself but my legs feel like they're jelly.

"Keep going!" Rourk yells behind me.

I hear him notch an arrow in his bow and watch his arrow soars into the air. He hits one archer on the roof. I go as fast as I can across the rocking bridge. Rourk fires another arrow and hits a soldier in the head. I'm amazed at his skill, given he is firing in the dark on a wobbly bridge, with enemy arrows raining down.

One arrow hits the rope where my hand had just been and I yelp, almost stumbling over the side. Rourk gasps sharply behind me. I turn to see an arrow jutting from his shoulder.

He grimaces and drops to a knee. I start to go back to him, but he waves a hand furiously at me.

"Go! Get away," he says through gritted teeth.

His furious resolve makes me stop. A burning rope snaps and the bridge veers wildly to the side. I keep myself upright by curling my arm around the supporting rope.

I have no choice but to keep going for the end of the bridge. Rourk gets up and begins notching another arrow, despite one still being in his shoulder. I thought he had hated me, but I can see how much he's trying to protect me. The determination in his eyes tells me he is every bit a good man as his brother is.

The boards begin to break apart beneath me and I reach the end of the bridge just as it begins to collapse, helped by the two soldiers waiting for me. I spin around in time to see Rourk disappearing into the darkness among the debris of the bridge.

"No!" I scream, falling to my knees. But there's nothing I can do. Rourk is gone, and his last act was to save me. Tears stream down my cheeks and I wipe them away as my grief turns to anger, which becomes fury.

I only have one option left. To confront my father.

Chapter Thirty

CLIO

"Father!" I scream into the night, shaking with anger.

I approach the building where he is standing on the roof with several soldiers. The two Oathlands soldiers are on either side of me, though I think they will do little to help if a fight breaks out.

The archers on the roof are readying more arrows. I see my father silhouetted against the fiery light filling the Oathlands. Markus De'Kalo, Royal Duke of the Kingdom of Aer. Brother to King De'Kalo. He is a powerful figure clad in armor, his helmet guard up, a broadsword strung across his back. It feels like months since I last saw him and the graying beard around his mouth. His familiar brown eyes, sad and strained. He steps to the edge of the roof, his armor clinking.

"Clio? Is that you?"

"It is me. I am here. Now, can you stop this madness?" I say, waving my arms over the town.

My father hops down onto a collection of stacked crates and hops again to the ground. He moves like an old man, I note, but he still has a lot of life and strength in him.

"My dear Clio, I'm so pleased to see you. Not to worry, these heathens will learn once and for all to fear the Kingdom's wrath."

"No, father. This is not what I want. This isn't right. It needs to stop right now. There is no need for war."

He eyes me like I'm insane. "What is this? Where is this coming from?"

My anger burns through me as I stand there, the wind whipping at my dress.

"You have no right to come here for me," I say, shaking with fury. "I know the truth, *dear father*. I know I am of the Oathlands. That you stole me as a babe. You *kidnapped* me. And hid the truth my entire life."

There is mild shock on his stern features, though it's not the reaction I was expecting.

"So, you found out the truth. In that case, let me be blunt with you, dear daughter. Do you really think we came all this way for you? This isn't about you, Clio. War may be triggered because of a person, or a crime, but it is a beast that is beyond us all. We must show our dominance over these Oathlanders. That is the way it has always been. And the way it always will be. Now, you are either with us or against us."

"You would kill the woman you raised? The girl who looked up to you and thought the world of you?"

"I love you, dear Clio. I always have, and I always will. Of course I do. You were the best thing ever to happen to me and your mother. We... we tried for a child, but she couldn't... there were complications. We were resigned to never being parents, despite how much we longed for a child. And then, when I saw you there in your crib, all alone, I knew what I had to do. You were so precious. And, yes, even though you were an Oathlander, I knew that raising you in the Kingdom would instill in you the grace and intellect of a natural citizen."

I almost feel sorry for him, and the sadness in his eyes reaches my heart. But his last words have riled me up.

"You think the Kingdom citizens are so pure and mighty. Like all others are beneath them. You're blinded by your arrogance. You don't even know what the Oathlanders are really like. They are good people. Better people than you."

He slowly shakes his head. "Dear daughter. They have corrupted you. How easily you will throw your life away. Leonas has been a wreck, not knowing if you lived or died. After everything I have done for you, this is how you repay me? Now, I say this only once more. You are with them, or with us. There is no other way."

"If I go with you, will you end this war?"

He scoffs. "If you come with me, I will let you live."

I scowl at him, my fists clenching. "You will watch them all die, won't you? You're a monster."

"That is the way of things," he says, almost sounding sad.

"I will not go back with you, Markus," I say defiantly.

"That is a shame. You would have made a great queen one day."

"You mean a great puppet."

He regards me for a moment before loudly saying, "Kill her."

The soldiers on the roof notch their arrows, and I tense. Oathlands soldiers on either side of me charge at my father with their swords drawn. The arrows from the roof find them and drop them. I scream at my father to just leave, but he laughs at me, which fuels my anger. My fists tremble and a burning, thrumming sensation churns through me.

A dark figure soars through the air and lands on the roof. I know instantly that the large man is Arthur. He moves swiftly between the soldiers, throwing punches and kicks like a whirlwind. I almost see him as the beast, but in his human form.

Markus De'Kalo watches with what seemed to be awe, but then tries to feign disinterest. Arthur dispatches the soldiers with ease.

"Clio!" Arthur calls out.

He leaps off the building and swoops down toward my father. In a flash, my father throws up a dagger. Arthur spins while falling and manages to knock the blade away with supernatural speed. But the second blade my father immediately throws embeds itself in Arthur's side. I cry out as Arthur hits the ground and lands in heap, sending up a cloud of dirt.

My father unsheathes the broadsword from his back and points it at me, causing me to stop in my attempt to reach Arthur.

Dozens of Kingdom soldiers are coming up the platform to us. There are so many of them that there is no way to fight them all, even if Arthur wasn't injured. Across on the next plateau, I see dozens more soldiers descending into the town.

"These people are actually trying to protect you," Markus says. "Fascinating. And foolish." He steps towards Arthur, who is barely moving and looks to be severely injured.

Seeing my fake father kidnapper standing over Arthur fills me with rage. My rage boils and the thrumming within me bursts. There is no way I can stop the power from exploding out.

I throw a hand up, and a jagged pillar of white light shoots up into the sky. Thunder crashes and rolls. I scream, letting out all my fury and hatred and bring my arm down, and with it comes fire from the sky.

White streaks of light strike out and decimate the approaching Kingdom soldiers, and those across on the next plateau. Their bodies fill with light and burn, and the ground explodes where the lightning hits, sending out showers of earth and flying bodies.

When the power leaves me, I collapse to the ground, on the brink of fainting. I feel like I've just blacked out, but I'm aware of what has happened. Somehow, that lightning had come from me. I look up through watery eyes and see that Markus is no longer there. Had I struck him down? I don't think so.

Cursing, I get to my feet to find him, but end up falling when my knees buckle. My body tells me to lie there, but I have to keep going. I must get to Arthur, who I hope is still breathing.

My father... my kidnapper... is gone now, and there's nothing I can do about that. A thick, ghostly mist is in the air, from the effects of the white lightning, along with the stench of blood and burned earth.

I stumble to Arthur, fighting against the exhaustion in my bones, and see he is still breathing. He's alive, but I need to get him medical attention. All around, I sense the shifting of battle. The Kingdom soldiers are retreating. My father must have called them back. As I lay there beside Arthur, the sounds of war diminish, though the tortured screams remain.

It's over. For now.

Chapter Thirty-One

CLIO

I sit by the window, pondering, and feeling safe in Arthur's tower. I've been in his sleeping quarters for the past two days, overseeing his recovery, and despite our trauma, it's actually been nice spending so much time with him in his room.

The Oathlanders have been slowly recovering from the devastation and their losses. The predictions are that over two thousand have died or are missing, and a thousand more are wounded. So much death. I can hardly fathom it.

Movement comes from behind, and I turn as he appears, holding a mug of tea.

"Six hells, Arthur. I thought you were in bed, resting."

He places the tea on a table beside my chair, wincing as he moves. I can't see it, but I know there are bandages wrapped around his torso under his shirt.

"I was, and then I thought it would be fun to sneak out. That's the only way I can leave this room, with you here guarding me. You looked like you could do with a tea."

I pout. "Well, you were right about the tea. But, please, you should be resting. The doctor said you shouldn't over-exert yourself."

"Well, that's a shame, isn't it?" he says with a sleepy, sensual gaze, looking me up and down.

I laugh and try to sound serious. "I mean it. You should be resting in bed."

He grimaces and lets out a sigh as he sits on the windowsill in front of me. "I heal quicker if I work towards getting stronger, not weaker. Laying in bed won't do me much good. Not with how much there is to do. Unless you want to join me, of course," he throws a grin my way before turning to the window.

"Well, you can't help anyone until you're fully recovered," I say, and realize I'm lecturing him. So I ease my tone and noticed how pensive he is, looking out. "Have they recovered a body yet?"

"Not yet," he says in a low voice.

We've had people searching the fissures for Rourk's body, but so far we haven't found him. Some have made up scenarios where Rourk could have survived the fall, but with his injury, I'm not so sure. Arthur is holding on to hope, and once he's healed enough, I know he'll be right down in the fissures and caverns looking for his brother day after day.

"How's May?" I ask. "Is she still...?"

"Still locked in her room. Yes." His deep voice is extra gravelly in his sorrow. "She's a mess. And I can't do anything to help her."

"She just needs time."

The poor girl hasn't left her room since the war ended. I've heard her crying sometimes when I walk by the door, but she refuses to let anyone in.

"It's such a tragedy," I say, "that she would lose both parents."

Arthur shoots me a fierce glare, and I apologize for my choice of words.

He shifts to face me a little more. "What about you? That was some lightning storm you conjured. Are you ready to talk about that yet?"

"I... I don't know. I still don't know how I did it. I think I might never be able to do that again. It certainly took all my energy."

"We'll just need to spend time training and exploring your power."

I nod, knowing he's right. I know what I must do. Even if I don't particularly love the idea of doing something as great and powerful as *that* again, I'll need to learn to hone it so I can control it and stop myself from exerting so much of my magic at once.

We both feel that the war between the Kingdom of Aer and the Oathlands is far from over. We must be ready to fight back. And now, I will fight on the side of the Oathlands. Never once did I think I'd feel anything more than indifference towards the Oathlands.

And now it is my home.

"And you're sure about what you said?" Arthur says, observing me. "About staying here? And all that talk about being an ambassador?"

"I don't know if I ever called myself an ambassador, but yes, I meant what I said. We will do what we can to convince the neighboring lands to help the Oathlands. They will share their resources with us and hopefully we can open shipping lanes between us."

"We've tried many times before to open trades with them. Why would they listen to us now?"

"Because now, you have the princess of the Kingdom of Aer on your side. They know me and they love me. Even if I now speak for the Oathlands, they will listen to me. My mother... my fake mother... was an ambassador. I picked up a thing or two from her before the illness took her."

He grins at me. "You just want to get your fields to tend to."

I laugh at that. "You've got me."

His eyes harden as he stares at me with a crooked, satisfied smile that reminds me of May.

"What?" I ask.

"Nothing. Just... thank you."

"For what?"

"For everything."

I look into his eyes, and I know exactly what he means. His trusting gaze tells me that I have shown him he can truly be loved, and I feel my heart swell with joy. "I love you more than anything else in the world. I love all of you, both man and beast. The thought of not having you by my side is unimaginable."

Arthur stands and takes my hands in his, pulling me up to stand next to him. He leans down to whisper in my ear, his warm breath sending shivers down my spine. "I love you too, my sweet allspice. More than words can express." His lips brush against mine, and we share a deep, passionate kiss that leaves me breathless. "Every moment I spend with you is like living a dream," he continues, his voice soft and tender. "I never thought I could find someone who sees me for who I truly am, and accepts me with all my flaws."

As we pull away, I feel a sense of completeness and belonging wash over me. I know that this man, my beast, is the missing piece of my life that I never knew I needed.

I resist the urge to push him into bed, knowing that rest is out of the question if I join him there. It's nice to stand there with our arms around each other, yet my heart aches as I stand there, embracing him tightly. I wish more than anything that all was right in this world and we could just spend time together in peace.

"So, what's next?" he asks.

"You need to recover, that's what. As for the town, they will have to do whatever they can to move on. And mourn their dead."

Arthur has that troubled look on him. His famously brooding face. "They're going to need me now more than ever, now that Rourk is gone. I can no longer be a recluse hiding away in my tower. I need to be among the people to help them, and be closer to the military. We all have to be ready for the war that's coming."

We have a lot to do, but for now, I'm going to enjoy being with my love and settling into my new home.

I hold him close and kiss him.

"And we will do it together."

WHAT'S NEXT

Thank you for reading *The Bandit Lord's Captive!*
Did this book give you all the feels?
Reviews are the high-fives of the literary world, and you'd be my hero by leaving one. Only a small percentage of readers take the time to leave reviews – you could be among that exceptional group who helps others discover the magic within these pages.
Plus, they make my day. So, please share your thoughts! Or even just taking a few seconds to drop a star rating is hugely appreciated! You should see one right about this point in the book....

- Alexa

Want to see what happens next? Be sure to check out

The Lost Guard's Healer, Book 2 of the ***Heart of the Oathlands Duet***

I am tasked with healing my sworn enemy. I would rather fight a wild boar bare-handed.
Nursing an injured soldier isn't my idea of a good time. Rourk is grumpy, stubborn, and entirely too handsome for his own good.

The Oathlander makes a terrible patient. Every order is met with skepticism or complaint.
But an oath is an oath. And in our forced proximity, I see the side of him that's surprisingly human—and occasionally funny.
He is everything I've been taught to hate, yet something about him intrigues me.

Maybe it's the hardened warrior showing me his soft side,

or the way he looks at me when he thinks I'm not watching.

The ancient magic returning to our world brings with it a threat that could destroy us all. Will we be able to put aside our differences and face this danger together?
Or will we all perish in the fallout?

The Lost Guard's Healer is a steamy forbidden love fantasy romance, recommended for ages 18+ due to language and content. It's a full-length standalone book with a happily ever after and no cliffhangers

---

Did you enjoy this book? Want to see more by Alexa? Then you'll LOVE **The Forbidden Royal Mates Series**, a completed series of 4 a full-length enemies-to-lovers, fake fiancé romance books.

Keep reading for a sneak peak of the first book, *Bargain with the Witch Prince*—

KELL

PRINCESSES AND DYING FATHERS

It is unseasonably cold this summer, but perhaps the chill is in my bones, not the air.

My steps are slow, even though I know I should move faster. What if this is the last time? What if he's going to tell me goodbye? It's something people think they want. One last farewell before their loved one slips away from them.

I can safely say that it is in no way better than receiving no word at all before they die. I've gone back and forth on what I would prefer. Do I want my father to tell me he's proud of me, that I'll make a fine king, before he exhales that last time? Or do I want my mother to come into my room at night, sniffling softly, explaining that he's dead?

I would prefer it if he didn't die at all.

I hesitate before pulling open the door to their bedchambers. Trying to look casual, I stuff my hands in my pockets and put a blank expression on my face, but my body is buzzing with frozen nerves. I don't know what to expect.

Relief floods my body as my father greets me with a small smile. It's nothing like the grand ones he used to show, before he got so sick even the healers couldn't do much about it. But in the weak one he wears, I see the strength of who he was before the illness. He's still alive.

I just don't know how much longer that'll be true.

"I know it's late," my father says, his voice gruff, hoarse.

Shrugging, I go to sit down on the bench at the foot of their bed. "I was awake," I tell him. "Do you need something?"

He and my mother, watching us from her favorite reading chair by the windows, exchange glances. "I'm hoping you'll do me a favor."

I nod, though I have no idea what I'm agreeing to. I can't think of one thing I would deny my father anymore, not now that his days are so numbered that it's a relief to know he makes it through the night. "Of course. What is it?"

"It's a big favor," He warns.

"If it wasn't, you'd have asked a maid to do it," I reply. "Tell me."

"I want to watch you become king."

I blink at him slowly. "Oh," I say. It's not what I expected, but it's not exactly a shock, either. My father has always been a sentimental man. "Of course. Whenever you're ready."

He smiles again, but it's more strained. A little awkward, which is something my father rarely is. "I'm sure you recall there are a few requirements for wearing a crown."

Frowning, I try to catch his meaning. "I kn—oh." I stare at him for a long moment, biting down on the frown that tries to slip free. "Have you found someone, then?"

He shakes his head. "No, of course not. You're free to choose which princess you marry, Kell. Should you choose to marry one at all."

He means if I choose to go through with this. To give him his dying wish.

It would be physically impossible for me to say no to him. And though I want to hold it back, just so he doesn't see how much this weighs on me, I sigh. "You know I'll do it," I say.

"Can't deny the dying old guy, yeah?"

I laugh, just like he wants me to. "Something like that," I say. "It's going to happen eventually, isn't it?"

"Your mother will have letters sent out tomorrow if you're okay with this."

I'm not. I'm absolutely not okay with this. The last thing I need is a bunch of princesses taking up my time while I'm trying to soak up the last of my father's life with him. "I'm okay with it," I lie. "It's what you want."

My father pats the bed beside him, a silent expectation. I stand from the bench, move closer, and take a seat right where he wants me. He grabs one of my hands in his and with his other, softly presses his fingers to my face. They tremble against my cheek as if the effort of even this simple action is too much for his body now. They're not as warm as they used to be, and they're clammy. It feels exactly like what it is—like having someone so ill they're nearly dead touch you. "What I want," he says, "is for you to be happy."

I give him a wry grin, hoping he doesn't see through it. "You're asking a lot now, old man."

He chuckles. "You're going to make a fine king," he tells me. "A good one. Make sure you find yourself a good queen, will you?"

"I'll pick the girl from the most powerful kingdom," I promise.

He shakes his head. "No, that's not what I mean. Perhaps I should say find a girl who will make a good wife. A suitable partner. Make sure you like her. Make sure you could someday love her. Find a girl who will make you happy, Kell."

I'd much prefer it if I didn't marry at all. There's a loophole that's been used before, but I know that if I used it, it would only disappoint my father.

And I refuse to disappoint him.

He stares at me as if he's trying to memorize my face. "It'll be hard to find a woman who can put up with me, let alone one who makes me happy," I say. It's supposed to sound like a joke, but I don't think it does.

"You are a good man," my father says to me. He taps his fingers against my cheek. "Anyone would be lucky to wed you. Just make sure you are lucky, too."

I nod. "Okay," I say softly.

My father drops his hand from my face and squeezes my fingers with the other. "Get to bed," he tells me. "You're going to have to rest."

"I need my beauty sleep now that potential suitors will be visiting."

He tries for a smile, but his lips only barely twitch. Exhaustion is written all over him. "Goodnight, Kell."

I stand up and give him a slight bow. It's a lot easier than speaking as I watch his eyes shutter close, watch him grimace as he shifts his body to get comfortable.

It's said that actions speak louder than words, which implies that it is far easier to say something than to do something.

I find that to be untrue. It is far simpler to lie with my movements than it is with my words.

JOULA

BIRTHDAYS

M y mother speaks to me as if the news she shares is something I don't know.

"Your birthday is coming up."

I merely nod at her and keep stirring the stew that's just barely boiling on the stove.

I can tell what she's going to say before she finally works up the courage to do so. It's the same thing she says every year, and yet it never gets any easier for her to spit the words out. "Your father will bring you the best of gifts."

"He always does," I reply, trying to keep my voice light.

"Far better than I can give you."

This takes me by surprise. It's a fresh addition to our annual conversation. I sigh as I set down the wooden spoon and look my mother in the eyes. "I don't care about the gifts, Ma. You're all I need. All I want."

"Still," she says. "You deserve more."

I shake my head. "I don't want more. Especially not from him. I would rather have no gifts at all than have to see him again."

My mother's eyes sharpen. "Don't you say that," she hisses. "You know he keeps tabs on you."

"Then perhaps he'll hear my words and finally get the hint," I bite back. "Dear Father," I call out to the empty air, "Stick to your own realm."

"Joula, no," she snaps. "That isn't funny. You don't know the things he can do."

I roll my eyes and use my magic to create shadows. They spill from my fingertips. I mime throwing them and push them toward my mother. When they reach her, they curl around her body before she scowls and bats them away. I grin before dissipating them. "I am very much aware of what he can do," I reply. "It's the same things I can do."

She just shakes her head. "I'm not talking about his magic." She looks around the room, perhaps searching for any sign of him appearing as if merely speaking of him for too long will summon him. "Is the stew done? I'm ready to eat."

I shake my head. "Not yet." I frown as I pick up the spoon and start stirring again. "I wish you weren't so afraid of him. There's no reason to be."

"There are plenty of reasons."

"He may be a demon prince, Mother, but you made a bargain. He can't do anything to you."

She laughs, the sound devoid of humor. "It has been nearly twenty years since I made that bargain, child. I can only imagine the loopholes he has found by now. Your father is a clever man."

"He's a cruel one."

"He is both, Joula. Do not forget that."

"It would be impossible to."

My mother is quiet for a long moment. It feels like she's waiting for the right moment to change the subject like she always does. I keep my eyes focused on the stew, waiting for her to decide what topic she wants to distract me with.

"I'm sorry."

I snap my head up, my gaze meeting hers. "What?"

"I am sorry," she repeats, "For what I did. For the world I brought you up in. I wish things could have been different, I do, but they can't be. I can't take back what I did, and I don't think I would even if I could." She pauses. "You don't know what it was like for me, then."

And she's right. I couldn't possibly understand what it was like to be her when she was my age. When she was younger than I am, even.

But I know the story.

Her name used to be Mijska before she changed it. Mijska was made an orphan at birth when her mother died, and her father had been killed at war six months prior. She was born in Csklokia, a country so fucked that its people will do nearly anything to escape.

Since Mijska was orphaned, she grew up in a large brick building with other kids who had no family. None of them were over thirteen years old.

Because the children were sold on their thirteenth birthday. Auctions, of course, to see just how much money the government could make off these kids. From the day that they learned to walk or the day that the children were abandoned in the orphanage, if they were older than that, they trained the children to be servants.

In all ways.

They taught the children how to do anything and everything that their buyer might want from them.

They sold Mijska to a man named Kizck Xurzk, a Lord of Csklokia. In public, he was kind. In private, he was wicked. He was kind enough, at first. As he took her home in his large carriage, he gave her space, introduced himself, and he told her about where she would live. When they got to his manor, he showed her to her room, which she got to have all to herself. Mijska wasn't used to privacy.

She never got used to it, either.

For the first few nights, while she settled in, Kizck left her alone. During the days, they sent her off to do chores throughout the house, which she didn't mind. She'd been cooking and cleaning her whole life at the orphanage—at least now she got her own room, a comfortable bed, and pretty clothes out of it.

And then.

Mijska was sleeping in bed when she heard the door open. It woke her up, and as her eyes fluttered open, she saw a tall man striding toward her, his footfalls silent. "Kizck?"

"Yes, Mij. It's me."

"Is it morning?" Mijska sat up in bed and adjusted the rose-colored silk nightgown she wore.

"No," he said. "You can go back to sleep after I leave."

Kizck sat down on the edge of her bed. His eyes studied her entire face before sinking lower. Mijska shifted uncomfortably and pulled the blanket up further over her body.

"Don't do that," he said to her. He took the blanket and pulled it off her, exposing her body. "I want to see you." He traced his soft hands over her body. My mother would say later how obvious it was that he had never done a day's work in his whole life. Her hands, even then, had been rougher than his.

"Kizck," Mijska whispered to him, "What are you doing?"

He chuckled softly at her before sliding his finger higher on her leg, under the hemline of her nightgown. He caressed her skin softly. "You're a smart girl, Mijska. Don't tell me you thought I spent thousands of ivzk on you just so you could wash my windows."

"You have a lot of windows," she whispered.

Kizck chuckled. "Nonetheless," he says, "I've got to make sure I get my money's worth, don't I?"

Mijska spent five years with Kizck as his little plaything and his servant. He greeted her almost every night after that, and she quickly learned that it was better to do what he asked of her than to try to fight back.

The opportunity to escape came on Kizck's birthday. The Csklokian king threw a party for his favored Lord in the castle, and he did not invite Mijska to go. Why would she be? So everyone would know just how terrible of a human he truly was?

Mijska escaped out her bedroom window, breaking her arm and one leg on the thirty-foot fall. It was her only option, considering all the guards posted throughout the house and the yard. She got up, and she ran on that broken leg, biting down on her tongue to avoid screaming. She even bit the tip of it off, but all Mijska did was spit it out and keep running.

Guards began shouting from behind her, but she bolted for the woods surrounding the house. They caught up to her quickly, so Mijska did the only thing she could think to do. She scrambled up a tree, nearly falling as she threw her broken body from limb to limb.

The guards did not give up. They waited for her to come back down, knowing that she would have to come down eventually if she were to try to get away.

She would rather die.

No one had taught to use magic, so that wasn't a viable option, but she could do one thing. One thing she had read about in a book and taught herself, in case she ever needed it.

Mijska summoned a demon with her own blood up in that tree. She didn't know at the time that he was a demon prince, but I'm not so sure she would have cared if she had known. They made a bargain: Safety for her and her lineage in exchange for whatever he wanted.

My father, Elix, healed my mother. He carved a place for her in Aligris, though a small one. And in exchange, he only asked her to show him what it would be like to love a witch. She should have asked for clarification, but after all she had been through, I suppose it wouldn't have mattered.

I was born nine months later.

My father stuck around for the first few months, just until the signs of my demon heritage started to shine through. I would create shadows or flowers or balls of light to amuse myself. And then he thanked my mother for this wonderful gift he had given her, kissed her on the cheek, and left us both.

He has visited once a year, on my birthday, ever since.

I have always hated him for what he did to her.

But, despite everything, I think she has always loved him for it.

Did you enjoy this sneak peek? Want to read more about Kell and Joula's love story, as well as 3 other forbidden love stories? Then you need to go NOW and grab the ***Forbidden Royal Mates Series***! You can also sign up for my newsletter here, get free books and be the first to know when my new books are released!

ALEXA ASHE
BARGAIN
WITH THE
WITCH PRINCE
A FORBIDDEN ROYAL MATES BOOK

ABOUT AUTHOR

I've always been fascinated by the magical worlds that exist only in the imagination. In fact, I once tried to cast a spell on my math teacher to make him forget about homework - it didn't work, but it did inspire me to start writing my own stories.

When I'm not busy creating new characters and stories, I'm usually snuggled up with a good book and a hot cup of tea (or a glass of wine, depending on the time of day). Just don't disturb me while I'm in the middle of a particularly juicy chapter - I probably won't even hear you anyway.

I'm inspired by so many things - nature, history, mythology, and the human experience, just to name a few. I pour my heart into every story I write, and I'm always humbled by the positive feedback I receive from readers.

If you've ever read one of my books, thank you from the bottom of my heart - it means more to me than you'll ever know!

Alexa Ashe

https://www.facebook.com/authoralexaashe

Printed in Great Britain
by Amazon